RIVER'S EDGE

When Valentine's gay friend Ryan disappears, she is reluctantly drawn from her island to the wider world where her rules don't apply. And for Detective Jane Stewart, uncovering a motive for Ryan's murder soon becomes more than routine investigation. But the river doesn't give up its secrets easily.

Cath Phillips' career has included being president of the Sydney Gay and Lesbian Mardi Gras, founding editor of *Capital Q*, then editor and publisher of *BURN*.

Other BlackWattle titles are reviewed at the end of this book.

RIVER'S EDGE

CATH PHILLIPS

BlackWattle Press
Sydney Australia
1997

With thanks to Gary Dunne, Lisa Mills, Laurin McKinnon and Carolyn Osterhaus.

Published by BlackWattle Press
PO Box 142 Broadway NSW 2007
May 1997

Printed by Southwood Press, Marrickville NSW
Distribution throughout Australia through Australian Book Group

Cover painting ©1997 David Collins
Cover design by Patrick McIntyre

ISBN 1 875243 25 9

For SGB

RIVER'S EDGE

PART ONE

Valentine

I am accustomed to great tasks. My island is a cliff, a bulwark against the river and my life on it is good. I live here alone. I chose this. I chose this island in the middle of the mouth of a great river where the water is wide and deep green. I am a recluse. This is my choice. This does not mean I am afraid of life.

Life is all around me and I like it. I like its hustling growth, its ravaged cycle of sprout, flower, die and sprout again. I enjoy the robustness of its challenge, its demand for strength and the flexing of muscle. It is people I detest.

I have built a fine house of timber and stone. Alone, with the strength of my own muscles, the tactics of my solitary mind. I have lifted and strained, carted and carried the materials of my sunny home. I have dug and turned, planted and hoed a garden that feeds me. I have animals that feed me and some that protect me. Life is a great task.

My river is eighty kilometres from the city as the currawong flies. No currawong in its right mind would want to fly to the city, to that brown muck that hangs in the sky like a cancer. Here the currawongs, both pied and black, whistle and scream their way through the skies. Huge skies, living skies, clean and blue, black and swollen with cloud, clear and sharp with light.

The river carries the sky's echo. The river is a great thing. It winds through sandstone cliffs until it reaches the sea. It is very wide and there are many inlets and streams, bays and beaches. Its true course can be difficult to follow. But now there are marks, cardinal marks and port and starboard marks lit with solar lights that flash in the night to guide the drunken weekend fishermen with their illegal catches, beercan detritus and plastic garbage floating behind them.

But do not think that because I do not like people I have no friends. Oh no, I have many friends. I have friends because I have an oven. A large, earth, warm-in-the-winter, cool-in-the-summer oven. And in this oven that took me two months to make, cure and christen, I bake bread. Fresh warm steaming fragrant bread, twice a week. This bread I sell to my friends. I sell goat's milk, cheese and yoghurt, salted pork and black-with-molasses hams. I sell vegetables and fruits that my friends are too lazy to grow. I am accustomed to great tasks. I feed the river.

I take pleasure in this activity. This is life, this is growing and dying and growing again. This suits me and my muscles. I can feel the blood coursing through my clean and glowing veins. It is rich and healthy blood, fed well and worked often. I am a large and strong person.

Today is my day for deliveries. I load up my tinnie and swoop around the river bringing bread and meats to my friends. It takes six hours to complete this task. The bread has been rising in the warm bakehouse, it has been baking in the glowing oven. I have orders to make up, lists to read and check. I start late in the night or early in the morning, take your pick. I like this toiling in the darkness. It suits me.

I know my fellow river dwellers by their appetites. Their loaves and fishes. They all pay cash. I have no credit to give. Weekenders pay extra.

My tinnie is a good one, broad and deep. It has no pretensions, no baubles, no shiny bits. Just scratches and dings, dents and dirt.

I find travelling on the river to be a fine experience. There is the wind and the speed and the water underneath. The horizon moves at a different speed to the water at the bow. I am Einstein — the world bends around me. The tinnie experience is a floating one. Really. The boat planes just above the surface, disconnected and discrete. Wrapped in the sound of the wind and the engine, I am solitary and complete. In control.

I take two dogs with me and leave the others behind. There are signs on the beach and the back bay, but people plonk their picnicking persons wherever they fancy. My dogs like strangers even less than I. They are good dogs. They do not like picnickers, water skiers, fishermen or drunks. They bite.

It takes six hours to do my run. West to Broad Reach, east to the ocean. I am salt-whipped and tired.

The last on my run are Ted and Ryan. They are my friends. They are old and happy in a homosexual union. I will say that again clearly and concisely so there can be no doubt, no obfuscation at a later date, no cleaning up, no ambiguity, let's not upset the family. They are old and happy in a homosexual union. They have been together since a romantic meeting in an illicit bar in the Cross in the early days of World War II. They did not serve, they were homosexual and in love. They ran away to the sea in a boat built for two and stayed there deep in the blue Pacific until the Japanese were bombed into submission and the world momentarily stopped killing itself. They are old and happy in a homosexual union. That means they fuck each other. Still. They are men after all.

Ted is waiting for me at his jetty. This is unusual. He is a bad tempered, dyspeptic old bastard whose typical conversation is a grunt. He gardens. In glory and joy he gardens. The soil is a canvas and his spade a brush. He makes compost so sweet and dark that we trade. His mouldering gold for my bread and friendship.

He has been waiting for me. He is agitated. He is picking at the skin around his nails, the flesh yellowed and flaking. The hair in his eyebrows is too long and sticks straight up. He looks demented.

"Ryan's missing."

This before I can say a word. The old bugger has practically climbed into my boat, his feet all over my baskets.

"Missing? What do you mean, missing?"

"He's gone, disappeared. I had a dream, a sort of vision. I think he's dead. Valentine, I think Ryan's dead."

Is he serious? He is. He is aged and wrinkled and terrified. I lift him out of the boat and place him back on the wharf. They need a new one. This one has been falling into the stream for the last fifty years. Maybe Ryan fell through it. I take their loaves and his fears up the slope to the house.

We drink tea. It is a grave situation. We drink tea from chipped and stained china in their dirty, cold kitchen. In his panic and fear Ted has neglected to light the stove and I have to do it for him. The room is damp and grimy. There is part of a kangaroo hanging from a hook in the roof.

He tells me his story. He went to town yesterday. Ryan was here when he left. There were no guests expected. There never are. When he came home last night Ryan was gone. Someone has moved their boat.

The boat is the *Annie Marie*. It's a Halverson, big, white and elegant, the only thing they ever keep clean. Brass rails aglint, green canvas pristine and neat. It's a big seagoing launch, a proud and lovely boat. It is locked up and secure, the keys hanging by the kitchen door, but Ted has looked. The fuel has dropped. It has been somewhere. The boat has been boating.

It is not in Ryan's nature to disappear without warning. This has never happened in all their years together. There are no friends for him to visit, no places to go, no ideas to have, no wishes to fulfil. There is no affair of a treacherous heart. They live here, up the creek, up a lonely and isolated creek because that is their desire. Their want. Ryan has not changed his wants in the space of a day.

Ted was on the train when he saw Ryan die. He had a dream, a vision, awake, in the daylight, as he sat there on the train. He saw Ryan falling through the water, he saw Ryan with blood teasing out from a gash in his head. Blood-red tendrils curling through the green water. Ryan was white and sinking down through the water. He was in the river. He was not breathing.

Ted is in pain. What can I offer him? What solace is there to give? What balm is there to give a grieving man? Could this be true? That Ryan is dead? Does an old man's vision constitute a fact? Does Ted's belief that Ryan is dead make him so? In the absence of evidence to the contrary, it appears that it does.

He certainly isn't here. Or anywhere, it seems.

We must find him. We must search and seek and we will find him. The river will give him back but where and when? I will tell the police. Ted doesn't want this, he is fearsome and trembling. Secrets, Ted? We are two and they are many. We must tell them. When he is found there will be questions and suspicions. Suspicions that will fall everywhere, nasty and distorting. We must tell them and we must find him.

Ted is gaunt and wracked. A violent hand has reached out and plucked his heart from his chest. There is nothing I can do for him. He is pain and fear. And today will not be the worst. He is alive and his love is dead. By violence, perhaps? At the hands of another? Alone. They are alone. One living, one not. What punishment is this?

He will not come with me.

I go alone to the police.

They may be many but the many are not here. One room, one desk, one sergeant. This is a tiny police place. A sub sub station, a child of Hornsby, the parent up the hill. The river needs nothing more, only one sergeant, only one boat. I tell Ted's story. The sergeant knows them, not well, of course, but she knows their place, she knows their boat. She takes notes on a pad. I am ready to fill out a form but she doesn't offer one. She is cautious about the prospects of finding him. Wonders if indeed he is dead. But she knows Ted and Ryan well enough to accept Ted's story for the moment.

It is a large river and she is one sergeant. Others will come from the city and look for him also. In their boat. Theirs is larger than ours. But they do not know the river well. Who knows the river best? I do. I will not go in a police boat. Even for a dead friend I will not do that. Nor for the living.

The dogs and I are in our boat. We follow the sergeant in her boat to Ted's house. Together we brave the treacherous jetty. She slips and I help her. He does not want us. She asks for the story I have already told her. He will not tell. He is withdrawn and tired. He does not want her here or anywhere. He wants to hide, tender and bleeding. He has lived with Ryan for fifty years. How can he be without him? Inside him is an empty, whistling space. Stop the clocks.

The sergeant gives up. She tries to hide the disgust on her face. The hovel, the pain, the dirt, the kangaroo. Too much, too old for her. She is a fine young thing. Ambitious and straight. Polished and pressed. What does she know of a hermit's love? The hours have passed, the sun is dying. The search will start tomorrow.

They cannot find him. They cannot find him for four days. Extra boats come from the city, their colours discordant among the greys and greens of the river. They surge around, blue and orange, high above the bow wave.

Uniforms are bright and sparkling in the sunlight. Pleasant blue overalls for the police, bright yellow and orange for the emergency services. They move in pairs, blocks of Mondrian colour.

Radios squawk and shout and yell. They cannot find him. They are well intentioned. They care in their semi-detached way. They have an offhand professionalism. They are conscientious and do their tasks to the best of their ability.

The sergeant marks her charts and listens to her radio.

On the third day she comes to the island in one of the big city boats. I watch as she ties up at the wharf and climbs up over the ridge. She looks around and calls for me. I wait for her to get closer, further across the side of the valley before I call back. She looks up and sees me in the stand of angophoras on the southern cliffs.

The dogs leave me and rush down towards her. There is barking, growling and threatening behaviour. She stops dead in her tracks. I let them get quite close before I whistle and save her.

When she finally reaches the top, there is mud and grease on the legs of her pants. A gum leaf is stuck to the stripes on her left arm. She slumps down beside me, tired. My guardians give her a good licking now they know whose side she is on.

"You've been watching the search from up here."

It's a statement, not a question. I wait for the next thing. She has come to me after all.

"We're not having much success. The river is so … I've never had a search in an area this size before. We are going to need help from the locals if we are to find him."

She gives me a long look and I give it right back.

"You know the river better than anyone."

The woman deserves an answer. She is trying her best.

"You don't know where he went in, or even if he did. Until you know that, finding him will be luck."

She turns her head away and gazes through the trees. The river is laid out before us, blue-grey today, the red in the cliffs muted by a scattering of low cloud. The hills roll back to the horizon, eucalypt-green.

A pair of white-bellied sea-eagles nests in the angophora we are leaning on. The male is sitting high in the tree above us, his head cocked, watching. The female is flying below the cliffs. Her wings are upswept and she is calling, a descending whistle followed by a harsh squawk. Catching a thermal she circles up, coming around beside the cliffs then soaring directly above us. We both turn, heads back, to watch her. She hangs in the warm air, her white breast gleaming against the clouds.

The sergeant is transfixed by the bird, head back, mouth slightly open, smiling. A sigh escapes her, wishes and dreams in one breath. She feels my attention and brings her gaze back to earth. Hopeful.

"Will you help … please?"

"You won't find him with those boats. He'll be tucked up under some mangrove roots somewhere. Somewhere that you can't get into. I'll look for him but not with you. How much more time do you have?"

"Another twenty-four hours then we'll have to call it off. He's not famous or anything."

"Have you seen Ted?"

She shrugs in irritation.

"He won't talk to us. He's just curled up and switched off. I knew they didn't have much but that place … Ugh."

She gets up to go.

"Thanks. If you find anything … "

I nod and she turns away down the hill. Up above me both sea-eagles are now perched on the same branch. They watch her go then the female takes off again, wheeling above the island.

You have to be smart to fool the river.

I dream about Ryan. I am driving in the country. The road is winding and narrow. There is a semi-trailer in front of me. I have the nose of the car close in behind looking for a place to pass. The truck is carrying cattle. They are red with white faces, Herefords, staring at me between the slats of the trailer. Packed in tight, they can't move except to raise or drop their heads. Some have their tails or hooves caught in the gaps between the rails. Their rumps and back legs are covered in dark green shit. I can hear them lowing over the sound of the truck's engine.

There is cowshit on the road and the truck's tires throw it up onto my windscreen. I turn the wipers on to wash, smearing it across the glass. I can smell the shit on the engine. The air is thick with it.

We are going up a hill. The truck is faster than I expect. As it reaches the crest, it swerves into the middle of the road. A lace monitor shoots out from under the trailer's axle. The truck has hit it. The huge body tumbles, turning on the road. In the space between the two vehicles I see the lizard roll onto its feet. Its head is thrown back. It is nearly six feet long, black and grey with white lacy bits. The front of the car strikes its neck so that its head turns towards me. Blood spurts across the bonnet and I hear the thump on the chassis as it disappears.

In the rearview mirror I can see it fly up into the air, turning over and over. Its legs are splayed out and contorted, its tail lashing in the air. It never seems to land. It just goes spinning round and round against the sky, legs and claws etched against the blue. Then it turns into Ryan with his face looking at me, blood running down his cheeks.

I don't like dreams like this. Who would like dreams like this? I am being pushed, pulled, and called. Nobody knows the river like I do. I bake twice a week. Tuesdays for the real people and Fridays for the fresh goodness the weekend wankers pay so much for. In between I will look for Ryan. I am smarter than the sergeant. I am stronger than the cops in their blue overalls and orange boats. I am smarter than the river. And the sergeant in her pretty blue uniform asked me to. This is a suitable task for me.

The kayak is best for this. It is closer to the water, quiet and sneaky. I can feel the currents when I am in the kayak. Pulling and twisting. Just a couple of hours today, out around the mouth of Porters Creek. He probably won't be there but I have to start somewhere. Better to start close to home. What if I paddle for miles and the old bugger is floating just under my nose?

This frail boat is a beautiful thing. It arrived one day by my jetty, there of its own volition, its arrival as silent and mysterious as a lost poem. The fibreglass is creamy, translucent. It has a sharp bow and high foredeck to cleave through stormy seas. Its antecedents are the skin kayaks of the frozen north. Together we make a hybrid child that rolls and cuts through the river's soul. In this craft I can live forever. In this craft I can hang upside down in the water, swimming and free. I can breathe the air or the water, the four of us are one. The boat, the woman, the water, the wind. There is nothing else but the next corner, the far horizon, the distance. The rhythm of the paddle and the ache in the neck.

He's not there today, just mud and mangroves sticky with plastic and beer cans. There's a mudflat just up past the cliff with the slip in it. He might be there tomorrow. The currents are never simple in the river.

I make lists of places he might be. They grow, each day. I keep adding to them. Places I've been and should go again. Lists in my mind. Turning them over and over. Running places through my mind like beads through the fingers of a saint. The currents are never simple. He may have been there, then taken away, brought back, dumped somewhere else. The days are adding up.

My shoulders are sore. Paddling all day is no easy task. I think I should start earlier. I am missing daylight by waiting for the sun to come up. If I leave the island in the dark I can be farther up the river when the light comes. The early bird ...

I'm only doing this because the old bastard won't let me sleep. Ted should be doing this. It's his boy's body. Ted can't do anything. He is a rolled up foetus in a fetid pile of blankets.

Some days I go out to the mouth of the river, to the sea. Just to check. The currents go down river as well as up. The water is different here. The slow, rolling, swelling sea. When I come out here it is difficult to return. The prow of my little boat stretches for the horizon. That great slow swell draws me out. I am riding the pulse of the ocean, the benign breathing of the water. Away, just away. The sea surges in my blood. One day I will go out there and not return. But not yet. For now, Ryan is stronger.

The dogs are driving me crazy. They are not used to being ignored but I can't fit them in the bloody kayak.

I haven't baked in a while.

My shoulders are sore. My back is aching and the bastard won't let me sleep. I keep dreaming. I keep dreaming that I am wet and turning over and over under the water. I can't see the sky, only a vaguely green patch which keeps receding above me. There is blood in the water. The blood reaches out and slips around me. It grabs my wrists and arms, pulling me down, twining about me in the brown water.

The kayak sits no more than ten inches above the surface. In this boat the river and I become the same brown fluid that pours between the cliffs. I am conscious of every current, every swing in the tide. I read the river through my wet bum, blistering on the seat.

Where are you, you stupid old shit? Just float up to the top and stay in one place. I can't play this game forever. My back hurts, my shoulders ache. My hands are blistered and my customers are complaining.

The weather is bad now but he still won't let me sleep. I can feel him tugging, pulling at the boat with every raindrop. There are southerly winds. The prow of the canoe slaps and hits at the waves. The wind hurts. It makes my forearms burn. Sometimes I feel like the boat doesn't even move. Stuck. I'm caught, held between the wind, the water and my own muscles. I can barely drive the canoe forward. He could be floating, right in front of me, swinging in the chop and I wouldn't see him. I keep going. If he was right in front of me then I'd run into the old bastard. He wouldn't escape.

I am losing weight. With every stroke a molecule of my flesh slides down the shaft of the paddle and mingles in the salt. My face has burned, peeled and burned again. My hands are cracked with salt. My knees ache with the soaking, the wetness seeping through the skin and into the joints like acid in the thread of a rusted bolt. The river likes payment for its little treasures.

The weather changes. Now the water is so smooth my little boat flies across it. Then the current shifts eighteen inches down and I am fighting through mud, pushing through muck. I flow one way with the tide then fight back against it. I burn in the sun then I freeze in the rain. I am always wet. The river and I are the same stuff. We roll and flow through the cliffs together. I can hear it whispering and laughing. Secrets so fluid.

Today the world is white. The fog is a different thing. I can barely see the end of the boat. Sounds are soft, strange as if only one speaker is working on the stereo. It is dangerous like this. I can hear the muted engines of boats passing somewhere in the murk. If they come too close neither of us will see the other before it is too late. Ryan could be circling, floating around me and I wouldn't know. But I have to be here. Sitting in this fibreglass shell has become my life. The boat, the water and I. There is no longer any separation between us.

When I drag myself from the water, when I balance my lovely boat on the side of the dock, I am bereft. My legs are dull, as stiff as an arthritic ancient's. I stagger on land with a graceless and heavy step. My island is an alien place. The return to the water is the only thing I crave.

I think I am going crazy. This was never part of my plan. This is not my life. Ryan has taken my life to replace the one he has lost. He is stealing my heart and the blood that is still in my veins. He wants mine. He has lost his. His blood has gone. Sucked out and swallowed by the river. Mixed and melded with the brown. I haven't baked this week. I didn't bake last week or the one before that.

He is down there tumbling somewhere under the surface. Swaying with the seaweeds, waxing with the new tides and waning with the old. He is melting, dissolving. There will be no parts of him left for me to find. The river likes payment for its little treasures. How much?

I think I am getting longer. I can feel my ligaments, my cartilage stretching and growing. Every time I dip the paddle in the water I am pulled a little longer. I am elongating. I am thinner. My muscles are going. Now there are only tendons and bones. Pulled so tight I could ping. I pong. I stink with sweat, mud and salt. My belly has collapsed beneath my ribs, moaning like an abused child. Is that what I'm doing? Am I remembering something I've forgotten to know? Psychoanalysis would be easier. I think I am forgetting to eat.

I can't stop the rhythm. Dip and pull. Dip and pull. My arms are motors, infernal machines. My eyes are searchlights, X-rays, infra-red. I can see beneath the surface. I can see through the mud. I am the mud. The mud is me. I can hear him calling me.

I am diminishing. I am disappearing in the water.

I've found him. He is wedged under a log lying with his face in the mud. The wood is sun-bleached and pale, damp and dark where he touches it. His shirt is gone and he is brown, blotched and bloated. The tide has pushed him under the log then swung him back and forth. He has pushed out a hollow in the mud, a shadow of himself. His shoes are gone but his trousers are still there. Thank heavens for polyester.

He doesn't smell. I thought he would. He is fatter than he used to be. The river has swollen him. Taken my flesh, my muscle, and given it to him. Fattened him with it.

I sit on the nose of the kayak, my feet in the mud, and stare at him. I'm tired. I've never been so tired in all my life. There are some rotted oranges and a VB can by his head.

This is no place to be left. The tide is receding, leaving mud up to my knees and I will have to drag the kayak back through it. Couldn't just be bobbing gently in the waves, could you Ryan? I have almost no strength left to pull the boat back to the water.

I have to go and tell Ted. Pull his yellowed stinking head out from under the blankets and tell him I've found his loved one. And the sergeant.

The river likes payment for its little treasures.

It is done. They are all told. The cops in their pretty clothes and bright boats have pulled him from the mud. Ted is back under the blankets. He stinks. His loss is eating him out like maggots on a carcass.

My home is a mess. A weed-ridden neglected mess. The dogs have forgotten who I am. I must take stock. The goats have eaten the young corn. The pigs have rooted up the compost piles. The cow must be milked again. The calf has been feeding off her. He is huge.

My oven is cold. Stone-cold and grey. I will weed the gardens and fire up the oven. I will set the sponge and bake. This will restore me. I will find my sanity again. In the earth, the animals and the yeast. Where it has always been. I will sleep. I will study the open skies.

I see myself in the mirror in my house. My eyes are changing colour. There are green flecks in the lower halves. They were not there before. The river is painting my eyes a new shade.

Stewart

"Hornsby's fished a body out of the river. Old guy — went missing five, six weeks ago. Looks like a bang on the head but no Path yet."

"Don't you know how to knock, Coburn?"

He grunts and stares at me. Nothing but hostility. Well over a year now and still he hates my guts. And all because I'm a woman. Some men are like that and most of them seem to be on the job.

"I've opened a file."

He drops the folder on my desk.

"I thought I'd go down this arvo and have a look. I've told them I'm coming. They'll need to get the boat out."

His tone is aggressive. He has a backlog of cases that he has failed to clear. He's always trying to get new jobs, easy ones so he can claim to be too busy for the routine work. Not this time, Coburn.

"I don't think so, sergeant. You have two ODs and the burning from Chatswood that you haven't reported on yet."

The blood rises up his neck. He glowers at me, trying to think of a response but he lacks the confidence.

"You don't have to stay in Homicide if you aren't happy with it, sergeant. It doesn't suit everyone. No one would think the less of you if you wanted to transfer."

He has been in Homicide for four years. He was my predecessor's drinking buddy. I shouldn't be doing this. He wants me to woo him, acknowledge his importance. I'm handling him the wrong way but he's a backbiter. A conspirator of the urinal. A lazy man who slips his work and mistakes onto the shoulders of others. Not with me.

He is clenched and angry. I can see the possible retorts running through his mind as he tries to decide which way to go. Discretion wins.

"I'm quite happy, ma'am. I know I've been getting a bit behind lately. A bit of trouble at home."

Sergeants are important. But he's not the only one I have.

"That will be all. You can leave the file."

His shoulders knot in anger as he closes the door. It clicks quietly. He hasn't the courage for real confrontation. I may be only a woman but I'm greater than he in both rank and stature.

Fifteen months now, I have been the commander of Homicide, Northern Region. The first woman in such a post. It has not been smooth sailing. There are no longer any girlie pics on the walls, the bad graffiti has gone and so have most of the malcontents. The office is clean, fresh with plants and most desks have terminals. The cleanup rate has risen and my bosses are happy. Coburn is mostly alone in his resentment. I have transferred his coterie of like-minded campaigners. His mates. In my view, mateship is a conspiracy of corruption, integrity drowned in a beer glass.

We have a body in a river. Identified by a friend as Ryan Porter. No family? What sort of friend? Edward Jones, resident of Porters Creek. Missing for nearly six weeks before he was found. Cause of death unknown. Possibly drowned. It's Friday afternoon and Coburn wanted to get out of the office, into the sunshine. So do I. Rank has its privileges.

It's a quiet drive down to the river, mostly through bush. Strange that it's so close to the city and yet so completely different. You could live down here and be totally alone, isolated, hardly ever see other people. I wonder if that was why Mr Porter was here. I wonder if he saw someone who didn't like him. Where's the family? There's always family somewhere.

Hornsby are waiting at the Police wharf. It is next to a large modern marina, dull grey concrete that has sprouted flags on coloured poles. A row of ancient date palms stands out against the eucalypts.

There are two officers in the launch, one a female sergeant. Alice Cameron. I am always recruiting so I watch her. If this job needs local knowledge, she looks like a good bet. I will certainly need an officer with water training. The other is straight out of Goulburn. He is cocky with youth and good looks. She is irritated by him and trying to hide it.

"What would you like to see first, ma'am?"

Cameron turns to me as she takes the boat out into the channel.

"Where the body was found, the person who found the body, the friend who identified it and Porter's home. In that order."

She gives me an odd look.

"Old Ted who identified him — they lived together — on Porters Creek. It was in my report."

She is wondering what I am doing here if I haven't read her report. There was nothing from her in Coburn's file. Damn him.

"I'm sorry, sergeant. I haven't seen your report. You can tell me about the case as we go."

The boat rises up in the water as we leave the marina channel. It is a clear day in late spring. The river is nearly three kilometres wide here. The chart on the fascia shows the ocean a few bends to the east.

Cameron tells me the story, shouting above the engines.

"About six weeks ago the woman who lives on Middle Island, just over to your left, reported Porter missing. Ted Jones, the guy Porter lived with, had come back from town and Porter was gone. No reason, no note, no plans, nothing. They have a big Halverson. Someone had taken it out and brought it back. The diesel was down. But it was all locked up again. Anyway, we looked for him and found nothing. Then Valentine, the woman who reported him missing, found his body on the mudflats out from Dead Horse Bay yesterday. He had been whacked on the head with something."

"Why didn't Jones make the report? He was the friend who identified the body."

We have come to a large bay, white sandy beach bordered by extensive mudflats. The tide appears to be out. Cameron slows the boat and we rock in the wake while she considers.

"The people who live around here are pretty eccentric. Most of them are hermits really. They don't have much to do with anybody else. According to Valentine, Jones had some kind of dream that Porter had been killed. He was so scared he couldn't do anything. He wouldn't make the report or help with the search 'cos he hates cops. Two old poofters — maybe he got beaten up in the old days or something. Anyway, when I went to see him after Valentine came in, he wouldn't talk to me. He hasn't since. He only identified the body because Valentine picked him up and brought him over. He and Porter have lived up their creek for years. Since the war, I think. They've got a shack, well, hovel really, with a bit of a garden. God knows what they live on."

Two old poofters. That may explain the absence of family and the withdrawal from the world.

Cameron points across the mud to a white log about a hundred metres away at the foot of a tangle of rocks.

"The body was under that log. If you want to go over there you'll have to wade through the mud."

She looks to see my reaction. They watch and judge just as you watch and judge. Every decision, every move assessed and reported.

I am afraid of water. A fear as visceral and real as vertigo. I believe that I will die by drowning, that I will slip beneath the deceptive surface and lose myself in depths where light never travels. The surface, so shiny, so real, will betray me, it will disappear beneath my falling limbs and I will die in an alien world.

I take off my blazer, shoes and trousers. As I do so, I can feel my heart rate increasing. Cameron gets the boat in as close as she can, the propellers stirring up the bottom. The water is brown and turgid. I step off the platform at the back. It is not cold but tepid. Death comes in a warm bath. I am in mud up to my thighs. My pulse is pounding in my ears, breath short and too fast.

There are sharp shells and tree roots in the mud. It is difficult and painful. I can feel a gash across my left toes. Halfway across the bottom becomes harder, sandy. Walking is easier now. There is blood oozing out of my foot. At the log the mud is deeper again, viscous and clinging. By the time I reach solid ground I am exhausted.

The two in the boat will see me sitting here. They will believe I am conscientious and dedicated, taking time to consider the circumstances of this death. The aftermath of fear is so debilitating I couldn't move if I wanted to. I still have to get back to the boat.

There is nothing to see. Some plastic rubbish, footprints and disturbance on the bank, probably from Hornsby getting the body out. There are scrape marks on the rocks. The hillside is thick with undergrowth and trees I don't recognise.

I turn and look back to the boat. Behind it in the distance I can see the ocean between the headlands. There are fishing boats, dots in the blue. The sky is almost white. It arcs over the sandstone cliffs, a few small clouds wisping their desultory way from west to east. I sit on the log and take in the view. Cameron and her constable are standing at the back of the boat.

This is a huge body of water. I wonder about the currents and tides. There are worse places to end up. But where did he start from?

Telling myself it will be easier, I struggle back to the boat, knickers and shirt wet with mud and water. The constable smirks as I haul myself back in. He probably hasn't seen a DCI in her underwear before. Cameron pointedly looks away as she hands me a towel from the locker. It is stiff and stinks of petrol and salt. I leave bloody footprints on the cabin floor as I clean up and dress.

By the time we get to Porters Creek I am dry again and reasonably tidy. The creek narrows as we go up. A gentle slope comes down to meet the water swinging around it. Under a rusted roof sits a small blue house. An extensive garden looks neglected and lonely. The bend in the river makes a lagoon on the other side of the point. It is heavily wooded, trees coming down to the water's edge.

The constable stays in the boat and Cameron and I step carefully across a rotting jetty. The paint is peeling from the house, cracking around the frames of two windows thick with dirt. The front door has been nailed up. The nails are too large and have split the timber.

I follow Cameron around the back where another door stands open. She calls out for Jones but gets no response.

It is a while since I have seen a place so filthy. An encrusted wooden table, an unlit wood stove and a rough wooden bench with a concrete tub constitute the furnishings. On the bench a blue china bowl sits, chipped and cracked, half filled with some kind of yellow muck that has dried and solidified. A drought-stricken custard. Cameron glances up at the roof. A water tank straddles two beams by a row of meat hooks, each hook surrounded by a dark brown stain.

I walk through the door opposite and into a dark corridor. One door to the left, one to the right and the boarded up front door before me. I go to the left. A double bed fills up a tiny room, pale sunlight struggling through the filthy window. The bed is piled with dark blankets. The room stinks of urine and sweat. The blankets are breathing.

"Mr Jones?"

I pull the coverings back. It's like removing the shell of a tortoise. For a moment I think he is comatose, then he blinks in the light. His skin is yellow and tight across the bones in his skull. He is curled up in a foetal position wearing striped blue pyjamas. I think they are blue. They are so dirty it's difficult to tell. I squat so my face is level with his and hold my warrant card so he can see it.

"Mr Jones, I am Detective Chief Inspector Jane Stewart. I have come to talk to you about Ryan Porter."

I could be talking to a corpse.

"Mr Jones, I need your help. I have to find out what happened to Ryan."

His hands are between his knees like a child's. He pulls them out and starts picking at the skin around the nails. It is thick and whitened around tiny patches of red. His thumb starts to bleed from a crack by the cuticle. He looks straight past me, eyes swimming in rheumy sockets.

"Mr Jones, I would like you to get out of bed. Can you do that? Ted, can you get out of bed?"

I reach out and touch him on the shoulder. He starts, and digs back under the blankets, releasing a wave of putrid air.

Cameron and I retreat outside leaving him to his muck and fear.

"Does he have any friends, anyone to clean him up? What's he been eating? Someone must be bringing him something."

"I don't know ma'am. Valentine, possibly. As far as I know she's the only one he'll have anything to do with."

"Do Social Services know about him?"

She looks uncomfortable.

"I don't know, ma'am. I haven't told them. I know he looks pretty awful but what would they do with him? They wouldn't let him stay here."

Here is a rotting hovel on the side of a mud-filled river. No power, no phone and fresh water apparently from a spring on the side of the hill via a black plastic pipe. Beneath the current chaos of the garden are paths and beds hinting at an earlier order. In the centre of the circular layout stands the remains of an old tree. The grey trunk stretches up about five metres covered in a green vine. Bright yellow flowers catch the sunlight.

Why did two men make this choice? Were they hiding from something or running to somewhere? Living up here may not be such a bad thing, self-reliant and unbeholden. Cameron turns her head towards the water and a moment later I hear it too. There is a boat coming. Fast. A utilitarian boat with a big engine and no adornment.

It swings in beside the launch rocking both of them. The wake creates a small surf that breaks on the bank.

She jumps out and slips through the police boat ignoring the constable. She is followed by a number of large brown dogs. They look as if they are all related. She comes up the slope very fast, is standing right in front of me before I can prepare.

She could be my twin. I am six foot two and her eyes are level with mine. She is two or three years younger, tougher and stronger. Muscles strung taut.

Her face blots out the sky as she leans in towards me, angry. Blue eyes are burning out of a brown cracked face. Her breathing is fast and deep. I join her rhythm. It's unconscious. We stand there squared off, breathing together, faces so close the edges of the world are blue and sharp. She smells like bread. A faint dusting of white pales the hairs on her forearms.

Cameron gives a small, awkward cough.

"Ah, ma'am, this is Valentine."

Of course she is. Who else could she possibly be?

I want to say she can trust me, I'm here to help, but all the platitudes taste sour and don't make it past my throat. Our breathing slows. The space between us expands, stretches, moulds the air with distance.

"I'm not going to hurt him."

"He won't talk to you. He'll only talk to me."

Her voice is fresh and slow. As if she doesn't use it that often. The tones were mine before rank and scepticism thickened my throat.

"I saw the boat come up here. I thought maybe you were going to take him away."

She doesn't like cops. What about this one? Step back and concentrate.

"Can you help me? I have to find out what happened here. There will be an inquest now that there is a body. I can try to force Jones to cooperate but I would rather not."

She fills the space I have just conceded. A blue-eyed animal, intense and absolute. Watching for me to slip up but I can play this game too. The thoughts fly behind her eyes like birds in a storm. I can spend the rest of the day standing here waiting for her to make up her mind. The silence expands, tense in the afternoon sunlight. The waiting game. No one plays it like a cop. We have all the time in the world. From the corner of my eye I see Cameron walking down toward the jetty, her back stiff. A dog pushes its nose into Valentine's groin. She gives in and starts to talk.

"Ted and Ryan were always together. They met during the war and ran away. They were a true pair ... some lovers are like that. You can't use the same rules."

She says it slowly, deliberately. The white cotton of her singlet catches the light and the flesh beside it glows. My hand comes up of its own accord and reaches across to touch the brown skin under her collarbone. It is hot and slightly rough. She leans into my hand, returning the pressure. The heat travels down through my wrist, along the veins of my arm.

Just like that, years of discipline and training disappear in the heat from the skin of a river renegade.

I could have this woman like an addiction, a pounding, hammering in the veins.

I am saved by gravity. My hand drops back. She laughs.

"Well now, isn't this a fine thing and I don't even know your name."

"I'm sorry. Stewart. Jane Stewart. I'm the head of Homicide for this area. That's why I'm here. You found the body."

I want to grab her and take off. Anywhere. Sunshine and blue skies. I want to smell her throat. Rub my face across her belly. She can see it.

"Yes, I found it."

There's something in her voice. How did she find it? Did she already know where it was? She turns her head towards the house and continues.

"Ted's a mess now. I doubt you'll get anything from him. Why don't you come back on Monday? I'll clean him up. Don't come here. He's not very good here. Come to the island. Just you. In the afternoon."

Why not? I certainly don't want to go back into that stinking mess.

She stays there on the slope beside the house watching as I go back to the launch. The constable has swung Valentine's boat across to the other side of the jetty. Cameron keeps her face carefully blank as she starts the engines and we drift out into the stream. The dogs rush along the bank, barking. The white singlet picks up the sunlight as Valentine turns and goes up to the blue house.

Valentine

After the madness, my breads are a poultice on a wounded soul. Flour, water, salt, yeast. Succour for the searching. The slow dark loaves are on their second rising. The sweet dough, dotted with fruit and gleaming with butter, is due for punching down. The bakehouse is warm with yeast and dusty with flour.

Every place needs its bread, every bread has its place. I am the river's bread. I slit the bags of flour open and pour forth their coloured contents. The plain white, the dusty tan of wholemeal, the beige of oat and rye, the silver of buckwheat and, best of all, the golden glow of durum streaming from the bags into the mixer's bowl.

I love durum flour. It is special. When my sharp knife parts the thread that seals the bags I feel good. When the yellow flour pours across my hands I am momentarily stilled, stopped, held by the light in the grain.

I spend much longer kneading the durum. I make a great loaf, a lovely bread from nothing but durum. Not many buy it. It is too strong, too uncompromising for those who like their bread filled with air. I make it nonetheless. It is the best. The dough begins grainy, pale yellow and harsh from the strength of the wheat. My hands, my shoulders, my back turn it to gleaming, creamy silk. It rises in a soft shiny ball that whispers of a deep burnished crust and tomorrow's toast. This is a bread for building mountains.

My dough tastes of me. My muscles have rolled it and punched it and thumped it on the bench. My hands have pummelled and pulled until it stretches and grows. My sweat has dropped sizzling on the oven floor.

This is a worthy occupation. There is no deceiving the yeast. We work together, the yeast and I. I feed it, it grows. If I feed it a lot, it grows a lot, but a faster loaf may not be a better loaf. The rich doughs. Ladies' bread. Dainties. The weekenders like these. French bread, Italian bread, German bread. I genuflect before the great bread nations of the world.

My routine has been interrupted by the dash to Ted's. I catch the fruit loaves before they outgrow their bowls. I have a long night's activity before me. This is good. The roll of the muscles fills the rhythms of my thoughts. There is dough to be kneaded. Rolls to cut and weigh. Trays to flour and tins to grease. There are three hours of labour before I light the oven. Three hours of not thinking about the woman on the river bank. The cop. The woman I have just met.

The oven is my own. My own design, my own labour, my own straw and mud, my own stone. Only the cement in the final slurry imported. It is mine. For my bread. This does not mean I won't share it. If you were to come to me with appropriate respect and ask to place your casserole, roast, ham hocks and soup in the dying heat of my oven I would be most pleased. But who would do such a thing with the microwave on the wall?

It is a beautiful oven, round and fat. The omphalos of my world. The centre of my island. It all ends here in my oven. The final process. The eggs from the chooks, the milk from the cow, the cheese from the goats, the herbs from the garden, the hams from the pigs, the rack from the vealer, the pie from the rabbit, the flour from the mill. Here in my oven. The transmutation of heat. The worship of food. And a mighty deity she is.

My oven is an outsider. The firebox is beneath the oven floor and is fed from the outside. It sits surrounded by its fuel. The stacks of timber I have cut and split. The fallen logs, the dead trees of the river end here, stacked in cords where the air can circulate and season. Chainsaw and blocksplitter are this baker's tools.

The fire burns, roaring and cracking until the grey floor turns white. I follow the heat as it reaches through the bricks to the door. When the white is edged with grey and just touches the third brick that sticks out slightly then everything is ready. In with the loaves and on with the door. By the time I have washed the bowls, refreshed the starters and cleaned the benches it will be ready. Then it cools while I rest.

As the sky lightens, I load my flour bags and baskets into the tinnie. The dogs are nervous. They remember the weeks of the kayak, the search. When they were neglected and excluded. Every time I leave now they rush the wharf, fighting for a spot in the boat. Big brown heads pushing. There is not enough room. Two dogs are all that fit and up the river we go.

Deliveries. The marina has the largest order, lots of dainties for the tourists and their morning tea. Sweet things for sweet people. Creams and chocolates. The weekenders clustered up past Broad Reach have croissants and rolls for lunch. Maybe a tart for dinner. If they think it's "pure" they'll pay twice as much. Lovely folks. Herb and cheese loaves to the tearooms then down river to my people.

Dark loaves and a treat for the shacks dotted in hidden coves. Salt pork, yoghurt and lettuces for two of them. It takes four hours to deliver that night's baking. There are fewer orders than usual because of my absence. "But you've been away, Valentine, I bought elsewhere." But not as well, did you? Ted is the last call. Lost, lonely starving-to-death Ted.

Now I think. I think back. Memory seduces and I dwell in the recent past. The woman on the river bank. Jane Stewart. There she was standing on the bank of the creek with her perfect pressed police persons. Waiting on the river bank in ambush. A trap for a lonely hermit. I gave her what she wanted. With barely a moment's hesitation I fell into her outstretched hand like a dropping plum. I told Jane Stewart I would give her Ted and she smiled at me.

What rashness was this? Swept away in the eyes of a woman as tall as I am. I told her to come to the island. I did this? The island is my sanctuary, the bulwark in the river, the castle that keeps out the world. I have dropped the bridge across the moat and raised the portcullis. Who knows what infection, what wild virus this will bring? A cop no less. A beautiful big cop with eyes the grey of a southerly squall.

Change and interruptions. Turmoil and outsiders. Killers who came here and killed Ryan. Murdered him and threw him in the river, blood washing from his head. Damn them. And Ted has become a festering foetus in a maelstrom of loneliness and fear. I don't want police and murderers in my life. I don't want tall grey-eyed cops in tailored trousers and silk shirts. But I gave in to her like a bending reed. She put out her hand and I bent to it.

Ted is barely conscious. The fug in the room is unbreathable. I pick him up, wrap him in one of his filthy blankets and carry him out to the boat. He weighs almost nothing and makes no protest.

I take him home.

I must wash him first. He is yellow with sickness, grey with muck. The dirt is deep in the canyons of his skin. There are sores on his genitals and buttocks, where the bones are too close to the surface. The stench rises from his body in waves. He hasn't seen a razor in weeks. A mess, a stinking suppurating mess.

The bath is too big to leave him in it alone. He will drown and there has already been too much of that. Ribs poke out from his bald chest. He was never that big but even so. His body has dissolved in loneliness. His toenails are extraordinarily long. There are scratch marks on his legs and ankles. A pale skeleton floating in soft water, eyes closed, nothing in his face. No words, no gestures, no resistance. A pliable ancient. Only a slow pulse to reassure me that he isn't already dead.

His pyjamas and the blanket I brought him in go in the firebox. Who knows what lurks in the seams?

Somehow I must make him eat. He is dried, powdered and wrapped in fresh linen on one of the dogs' beds. They are clean and they keep him warm. Their heartbeats match his, brown eyes watch his chest rise and fall. Canine nurses.

His eyes flicker open with a sharp slap on the face.

"Come on, Ted. You have to eat."

Soup spooned through dry lips. Most of it goes down his chin. Large pink dog tongues claim the lost drops, licking out his beard. Try again. And again. Eventually he swallows. More. I manage to get almost a cupful into the old bugger.

An hour later we repeat the exercise, this time with stout. My own stout, dark and creamy. The best thing for a wasted body. Some ancient memory in that fissured head must be triggered. The stout goes down faster. Swallows greedy.

Every hour I feed him. Soup and stout. He wets himself. I wash him again and clean the bed. The dogs look puzzled. Sniffs and excitement. This time I wrap a towel around his genitals. A makeshift nappy. I wake through the night, still pouring nutrients into him. Towards morning his head is pillowed on a dog's ribs, gentle snores vibrating from an open mouth. His colour is better. We both sleep until the day is warm.

In the afternoon I wrap him in a rug and put him in a deckchair in the sun. I can see him as I work in the garden. He sleeps, head drooping to one side. Rosie, one of the young bitches, has adopted him. She sprawls beside him on the grass, getting up every few minutes to stare intently at his face. She drops her glossy head onto his shoulder, sighs then flops back down.

I am late with my plantings. The search for Ryan has left my garden weed-ridden and fallow. I should have tomatoes, potatoes and sweet corn in by now. There should be neat rows of lettuce seedlings ready to replace the current crop. Broad beans and sugar peas should be harvesting. There is nothing but a row of stunted peas collapsing under powdery mildew.

I dig. I dig and dig again. My rock in the river has no soil. Only sand and rocks, rocks and sand. The soil I do have is that which I, with these muscles, these hands, this aching back, have made. Manure and compost, compost and manure. I got the cow because I wanted her shit before her milk. I got the pig to drink the milk from the cow and thence more shit. I got the chooks because scraping out their run is easier and cheaper than hauling bags of Dynamic Lifter up the hill. The goats and the rabbits because they are efficient converters of feed.

Some of my beds are over ten years old now and the dirt is just beginning to look the way it should. Deep, black and crumbling. Moist and dark. Alive with activity, millions of microbes multiplying. Dirt. Every child should be given a piece and taught to keep it alive. Black dirt. The richest stuff in the world.

I like gardening. I like the toil, the hopefulness of it. The chance that the tiny seeds I scatter about may grow into plants. Large plants with food on them. Small plants that scent the air. The optimism of plants that take root and grow here on a rock in the middle of a river.

I like to look at my beds, their stone walls warm in the sun. They are there because I put them there. I have moulded and shaped this hillside. And with no more than myself. No earth movers, no bulldozers. None of that here. Every stone sits where it does because I placed it. I sat it on top of and under its fellows.

I like to garden. It is a positive and powerful process. The city holds gardens that have become disregarded, bereft of care and soul. Gardens that are no more than a signifier of rank, an indicator of prestige. Another room to hold the latest in wicker furniture. Or just a yard of rubbish and riotous weeds. City people.

Does Jane Stewart have a garden or is her life only real in some heated and cooled office? Behind glass, behind a desk, behind telephones and keyboards. In the electronic networks of the modern police force. The thing about gardening is the tendency for the mind to wander. For other thoughts, unbidden and unwelcome, to come slipping through the day.

As the light begins to fade, I lift my shrivelled ancient out of his chair and take him back inside. Walking through the house I turn my head. His eyes are open and staring at me. Red-rimmed and rheumy. The whites milky as a half-poached egg.

Back to his dog nest. Rosie collapses her massive weight beside him. Good dog, big dog, strong dog. She pushes her head under his arm. His face falls to hers. Her wet tongue rearranges his hair. He submits to her ministrations. She grooms him like a pup until he is arranged to her satisfaction. She pushes him back in the bedding and stretches out beside him. She has the worst snore of all of them.

I milk the cow for him. Fresh foaming milk poured into him. He needs it more than the calf does. I must slaughter that calf this week. He was an autumn calf and is too big for his mother who should be drying off about now. More soup, more milk, more stout. He stays awake now, skeletal hand resting on Rosie's head. He manages to eat some bread by himself.

By Sunday afternoon he is back with us. His eyes are clear and he is awake and thinking. I tell him about Stewart coming tomorrow. He turns his head away from me. He is still lying in the dogs' bed with Rosie. She licks his face in sympathy. I try to get some acknowledgment from him. I don't want him switching off again.

"Ted, you are going to have to talk to them sometime. Better here with me than in some disgusting police station somewhere. Stewart will arrest you and charge you with something, you silly old bugger."

He ignores me and pats his dog friend on her head.

"You can't just turn off and hope everything is going to go away. Don't be stupid. You've just given up, you old shit. You think Ryan would want that? You think he would want you to just curl up and die because you're too pathetic to do anything else? You're a stupid, bad tempered, weak old shit and I've got a good mind to take you back and leave you. Who cares if you starve to death? Ryan isn't here to see it, thank heavens."

Success. He glares at me and splutters.

"How would you know what Ryan wants? You just go away. Go away and take the bloody cops with you. I don't want your help."

I drop down beside him and pick up his hand. It weighs nothing.

"Ted, you have to start thinking. Ryan was murdered. Someone hit him on the head and killed him. The police will try to find out who. The first person they will suspect is you and the second will be me. That's because they have no imagination, and most people get killed by someone they know. You have got to talk to them or they are going to make things bad for you. It's one thing starving to death in your own bed. It's another doing it in a police cell. Think about it. The sooner you talk to them the sooner they will leave you alone."

He is really too weak to resist. A great sigh pushes up from his diaphragm and nods his head for him.

"I don't suppose I can stop them anyway. But don't think I'm grateful."

He turns and wraps skinny arms around Rosie, sobbing. He shakes and shudders with sobs. The pain and loss come boiling out of his body. He is wracked with spasms. Rosie submits, her coat wet with snot and tears. I put a blanket back over him and leave him to cry. Rosie is better at this than I am.

I sit and wait. Wait for that woman to come. There has never really been anyone else here but Ted and Ryan. Apart from the sweet sergeant's visit during the search there has never been another woman here. A tall and grey-eyed woman. She is coming here tomorrow. She will stand in this room and turn that grey-eyed head to see. To see? To see what? What will she see here? How can I know? I sit and wait for her invasion like a whore with legs apart.

Stewart

Coburn is bleary-eyed, his face swollen and puffy. What does the man do with his weekends? He blusters into the room, anxiety and aggression at war in his body. Anxiety wins a close battle.

"Morning, ma'am. I heard you were setting up the team for the Porter killing."

He wants to be included but is unsure what weight I am giving to this case. I wonder about Cameron's missing report. I don't want him here. His violence and bigotry are no assets and if I was kinder I would put him out of his misery. I should send him away to some medium-sized patrol where he can shake down the local dealers and maintain what he knows as dignity. But I want him to suffer for suffering is knowledge. I want Sergeant Mick Coburn to learn that there is no place left for his kind. He is my reminder, the piece of darkness in the corner, the shadow that marks the light. But not on this case.

"Your workload is already heavy, Sergeant. This is not going to be a big case."

"Right then. I'll have the report on that Chatswood burning ready for you this afternoon, ma'am."

He backs out of the room, both relieved and resentful. I turn back to the two constables opposite.

"I've already seconded Sergeant Cameron from Hornsby. She knows the river and we need someone who can drive the boat. I don't remember any water qualifications in your files, gentlemen."

Eager faces, young and ambitious, happy to be working with me. They believe I will take them somewhere exciting and prestigious.

Sam Nguyen is first generation and has no desire to work in his own community. "I see them every day," he says, "why would I want to work with them as well?" He despises Coburn as one of the corrupt racists who used to pull him over and beat him because he was a Vietnamese kid. Sam's ambition is a hard fire that burns in his dreams. He wishes only to work.

Jamie Orr is his Anglo twin. Same height, same build but blonde instead of dark. They do Tae Kwon Do together, falling and striking, unified by the desire to succeed. Orr reckons that most cops are dickheads.

"Sam, I want you to go down to the marina and meet up with Cameron. Do interviews with all the locals that you can find on the river. See if anyone remembers seeing Porter on the river the day Jones was in town. See what people have to say about them, the usual."

"Do you want me to talk to Jones?"

He's eager.

"No. I'll be down this afternoon. Ask Cameron to meet me at the marina at two. After she drops me off at Valentine's I want you both to look at the Porters Creek place. Give it a good going over.

"Jamie, I think there's family somewhere in here. Even if they were two old guys who had opted out of the world, there has to be family somewhere. Get on the computer and find Porter's birth registration. See if his parents come up with any other children and trace them. Do them both for drivers' licenses and see if COPS has got anything on them. And get on to Pathology. I want the report by lunchtime."

Castor and Pollux. They are out the door and away.

Dogs cover the wharf, barking, frantic with excitement. She stands in the middle of them, a tall rock in a brown heaving sea. The island rears up behind her.

Cameron, in overalls and smiling, leans over and grabs a bollard, holding the launch long enough for me to clamber out and into the mass of dog. Despite the noise they don't seem to want to hurt me. My hands are licked, crotch sniffed and legs rubbed by heads that leave short brown hairs in the fabric of my pants. Cameron waves and roars off.

Valentine smiles at me, almost shy. Today's singlet is dark blue and she is wearing shorts despite the clouds gathering. The tension seems to have gone from her body, she seems softer, more rounded. The tendons and ligaments are no longer taut on the surface.

"Ted's in the house."

She gestures behind her up the hill. I follow where she leads. We are escorted by the pack, quiet now but no less busy. There must be a dozen of them. They run back and forth, noses in everything, tails wagging. They seem an extraordinarily happy bunch of dogs, but I'm no expert.

The slope is deceptive. We climb a small ridge and then descend into a natural amphitheatre. The small valley is a garden. Cultivation covers most of the floor and then rises in sandstone terraces up the sides. Sandstone is everywhere, in the walls, in the edges of the paths.

There are vegetables and flowers, beds of straw, scent and colour. The land that isn't garden is pasture. A golden coloured cow grazes with a large calf. A pig is rooting around in a pen with a shed in it. Goats and chickens scratch around a barn, its walls half stone, half timber.

At the top of the ridge, framed by twisted red trees, blue gums, and rock piles, is a house, glass and timber. It looks out across the sweep of gardens and paddock to a stand of casuarinas down on the shore. The river shines beyond the trees. The trees hide all this. In a boat you would never know it was here.

It evokes nothing so much as a European painting of a nineteenth-century colonial landscape. An idealised and bucolic scene. Everything is orderly, tidy, neatly put away. Nature not tamed but contracted with. A partnership, a symbiotic relationship for mutual benefit. She is standing on the path watching me. Hesitant, nervous for my reaction. What can I say?

"It's beautiful. Remarkable."

She smiles again.

"Apart from Ted and Ryan, you're the first person to really come here."

"I'm honoured."

No one ever comes here? To see this? She does it all for herself, all this work? Madness or determination?

We walk along the side of the slope and up to the house. It rises up against the sky, glass walls framed in timber. In front of it is a large stone flagged area leading to a smaller stone building with a large white dome at one end. There is a chimney behind the dome. It must be some kind of oven.

Inside, the house is spotless, light years from the hovel at Porters Creek. Polished wood floors, those soaring windows and books. Books everywhere, almost all the wall space is covered in bookshelves. Despite the overcast day, the house is warm and light-filled.

The purpose of my visit is lying on a sort of platform. There are blankets around him and yet another dog has its head resting on his thigh.

His health has improved markedly. His unshaven cheeks are of good colour, his eyes are open and watching. Tense. He carries the tension of the liar. He is going to tell me untruths and hide information like nuggets of gold. He knows what I want and is going to withhold it.

Valentine introduces me to him, shy and diffident, a virgin at her first dance. I am easily distracted and have to tell myself that she is not the reason I am here. She is not the main game in this room. I forsake her smooth limbs for his gnarled frame.

I ask him to tell me how he and Porter came to live here. What brought them together and why in this place. He relaxes. The secrets are not in the distant past.

"It was safer here. We came back after the war was over. See, Ryan used to come up here when he was a boy, that's how he knew about it. The river and that."

There is a strange quality to his voice — querulous but somehow fake. As if he wants me to think he is weaker than he is.

"We'd gone away … when the call-up came. We hadn't known each other long. We met at the Cross in 1940. Ryan was older than me and he used to go to a club up there. A club for fellas like us, you know."

The head ducks and he flicks a glance to Valentine. She nods. I do indeed know.

"I was too young. They wouldn't let me in. Not by myself anyway. Ryan sees me on the street and we start talking. He was attractive, you know. Handsome. I liked the look of him. He was strong. Not furtive and ashamed like some of them. Anyway we got together and it was right. But we couldn't join up or anything. They would have parted us and Ryan had already been beaten a few times by the cops up there. At the Cross. The cops there would beat us. It was all corrupt. Pay offs and such. The cops were part of it. They ran the Cross in those days."

Looks at me straight, defiant.

"Probably still do. People were … they hated anything that was different … There was nowhere for people like us to be safe … comfortable, treated ordinary, you know. Ryan didn't believe in the war. He didn't see why we should die for our country when people hated us anyway."

The wounds and longings of two young lovers, rejected and angry. The dog mimics his actions. When he sits forward so does she. When he sits back so does she. I assume it is a bitch. To my naive eye, there is a female cast to her head.

"Ryan had a boat. He could sail. It was a wooden ketch. So we took off. We just sailed out of the harbour and away. We stayed away for the rest of the war. In the south. Across to South America, through the islands, remote coasts. We hardly ever saw anybody. Just enough landfalls to get fresh food and water. It was good. We never saw any of the war. The warships and such didn't come down that far. We had some bad weather but there was usually somewhere to shelter. In those days people didn't know much outside their own area. No radios or anything. Just people, isolated like us. Helpful. Not like now.

"Anyway, we found out the war was over when we were in Chile the last time. We sailed back. Ryan wanted to get off the boat. So did I really. I wanted a garden. That's what we used to talk about, see. The garden we were going to have. What plants we would grow, the landscaping. He remembered the river. So we sailed in here. No one knew where we had gone so no one knew we were back. No one knew about us. It was better that way.

"We built the house on the creek and stayed there. Been there ever since. The garden never really got to be that much. The soil's no good up there. Valentine made her garden out of pig shit. I don't know. We got tired. There didn't seem much point in doing more than we needed. I suppose we could have done ... But we were happy. We were happy and now he's gone."

There is aggression now. Defiance, as if I'm to blame.

He doesn't seem to want to tell anymore. He is tired. He lies back in his blankets, the dog with him. He is so much cleaner. Valentine must have soaked him in bleach. My turn to talk.

He turns his head away from me. Questions are obviously unwelcome.

"The land you've been living on — who owns it?"

A quick flick in the eyes.

"We do. Ryan and me. We own it."

"When did you buy it?"

"Ryan did. He had it before we left. Before the war. He already owned it."

"He must have only been in his very early twenties. Unusual to own land at that age, don't you think?"

"No. He had money, see. A lot of money."

"And where did this money come from?"

"He inherited it. Quite a bit there was."

"Where is Ryan's family now?"

This is it. This is the bit he doesn't want to share.

"There isn't any. They died. He only had a brother and he died. In the war. He's dead."

Perhaps. Perhaps not. Money and family. Reliable killers.

"What did you and Ryan live on Ted? You've been up the creek there for a long time. You must have some sort of income."

"Investments. Ryan made some investments. I'm tired. I've had enough. You can't keep questioning me like this. I've been sick. Valentine?"

He looks to her for help but she doesn't respond. She is watching me not him.

"It's all right, Ted. I won't take much longer but I need to know what happened the day Ryan went missing. Why were you in town?"

"Just regular. I go up to get things every now and then. Supplies, you know, salt and stuff."

"What sort of things did Ryan invest in? What companies?"

A twitch.

"I don't know. We didn't talk about it much. BHP maybe."

"Was Ryan expecting anyone?"

"No. No, we didn't have visitors. Who would we want to see?"

"What happened to the boat you went away in? Do you still have it?"

"After all this time? No. Ryan sold it and we bought another … well, we had another boat for a while."

"And the Halverson? When did you get that?"

He goes pale. Valentine intercedes. She knows about the boat being used.

I take the search warrant from my jacket pocket and drop it on the bed at his feet. He looks at it, puzzled.

"I have two officers up looking at the *Annie Marie* now. They are also going through your house."

Anxiety flows out of him. The warrant flutters in his hands but he doesn't read it.

"Nothing … there's nothing. All our boats have been called *Annie Marie*. But there's nothing … Ryan wasn't on it … there's no connection with him being killed."

"That's okay then. We will have a look and if we don't find anything it'll be out of the picture."

"Go away. I've had enough. You can't ask me anything more. I don't have to tell you anything."

He is burrowing down under the blankets again. His head disappears. The dog tries to follow him but he's got the coverings pulled so tight around him that she can't get in.

I go outside and stand on the paving stones. The gardens are laid out before me. I can see the river and the entrance to the creek. The clouds have built up, dark and heavy with rain. Valentine is standing behind me.

"He tried. I've never heard him say so much at once before. You mustn't blame him. He's not used to people like you."

I turn and look at her.

"He was most cooperative."

Her eyes narrow. She fears my suspicions, is convinced I hold them.

"What is going to happen now?"

"I will need to talk to Ted again. Is he going to stay here with you?"

"I don't think so. We aren't that used to being with each other. When he is strong enough I will take him back. Rosie will take care of him."

"Rosie?"

"The dog. She's adopted him."

I was right. A bitch and I know little of dogs.

For a moment we both stand and look out across the island. We turn towards each other at the same time. What can we say? There is too much and too little. I find her overwhelming here, the island, her gardens and animals. She is too rich, too strong for me. I am still partly back with the old man. She could wound me with a sweep of her hand. I would succumb, crumble before her, all restraint dissolved.

"I will have to do a formal interview with you. Not now, this is not the time. I will come back tomorrow."

"No. Please, I will be baking tomorrow. It wouldn't work. Wednesday morning would be better."

Dammit. I'm the one with the authority. This is supposed to happen at my convenience not hers. She spreads her hands wide, a supplicating gesture.

"I'm sorry but I lost so much work when I was looking for his body. I couldn't miss another baking ... It's my livelihood."

I steel myself.

"A police officer will be here to talk to you in the morning."

A long moment while she considers her options. A shrug. She is practical.

"I'll take you back if you wish. It's no trouble."

I turn to go inside but her hand reaches out and she stops me.

"He won't hear you. He's gone back inside himself. I'll tell him you will want to talk to him again, later."

I could just stay here, standing, her hand on my arm. She has touched me, reached out of her own accord. I am stupid. There is nothing in it but a desire to protect the old man.

We go back down the hill to the jetty, dogs following. As we reach her boat thunder rolls. She looks at the sky and laughs.

"We're going to get wet. Do you mind?"

The old man's paranoia and fears drop from me. I am released by the laugh of a wild girl and the huge drops of rain spotting my shirt.

"No. Of course not."

I am lifted into the boat on a tide of brown bodies. They deposit me at the front and lick the water on my face. It is pouring now, as fast and furious as it came.

We fly across the water. The boat is open, no cabin, no shelter. My anxiety about water is momentarily defeated by the force of our passage. The wind drives the rain hard against my body, stinging. She stands up at the back, head turned to the sky, eyes slitted against the force of the water. I have never seen a face so sure, so clear. Her beauty burns in my chest. The rain has lashed the singlet to her body. Breasts in clear relief, muscles defined and shining wet. What am I to do? She is a suspect.

Valentine

I have returned Ted to his hovel home, Rosie trotting behind. He is strong enough now, flesh back on his bones. They have been and taken the *Annie Marie*. A policeman came to talk to me. I met him at the wharf. I don't think he liked me. I don't have to deal with her minions just because she sends them.

I am anxious. It flows through my body like fever, disrupting my day, my thoughts. This whole thing is bad. It is a situation, an event which I cannot control. The outside is so close. It comes with her, with the soft blow of her breath, the sheen of her skin. She brings the outside in the folds of her expensive clothes, in the faint air of her perfume.

I want my old life back. I want to see Ryan laughing on his rickety wharf. I want to bake and not think, garden and not pause, weed in hand, lost and lonely in thoughts I have never had before. I hold my loneliness about me like a cloud. I have always done this. It has been a comfort, a friend to me. This was my life, no one else's, mine alone and mine. But longing is the salt of loneliness. It brings a fresh and bitter taste. I am used to the bland starch on the tongue and now she brings a change. The heat of desire. I am caught. The fire burns away my anger. I dream instead.

She's as big as I am. Bigger at the moment. There's not as much of me as there was before the river took my flesh for that bloated body.

I want to see her here sitting next to me. A fine and beautiful thing. She doesn't know the river but she will. I'll take her nice and slow. Easy, so she doesn't scare.

You never know, do you, when it's going to happen? Here's me, living alone and crazy all these years. Just me and the dogs and the cows and the cats and the pigs and the chooks and the goats and the rabbits and the yeast then all of a sudden, up she pops. Out of the river. Did she slide her long legs into my river? Did she feel the cold mud slipping up her thighs? I want to warm her and dry her. Wash her in rainwater, scented and foaming. Wrap her and dry her in great soft towels. Lie her on the bed and fold myself around her. All soft and moist. She will come to me. I know.

Stewart

Rain is sheeting down the surface of the tinted windows in my office. The day is dark and depressing. The overhead lights are reflected in the waxed surface of my desk. I will not tolerate sloppy cleaners. Different coloured manilla folders are neatly arranged in front of me. Each colour denotes a different section of the case. Pathology is blue.

Ryan Porter suffered a heavy blow to the head. He then fell or was pushed into the river. He was still alive when he hit the water but dead shortly after. The blow to the head left the impression of a fifty millimetre spanner in his skull. No detritus was found, no tiny fragments of residual material, oil, grease or paint. Six weeks in the water have washed him clean. But the shape of the spanner is clear in the X-rays of his skull. Sharp and bright. A somewhat unusual tool. Probably made for a specific piece of machinery. The diesel engine of a large boat, perhaps.

Interviews of major suspects are red. Sam Nguyen had limited success with Valentine. His report is short and terse. She met him at the wharf and would not allow him any further. With all those dogs, who would argue? He describes her as "hostile". I find his dislike of her a relief. It is always a burden, to like a suspect. I do not *like* Valentine. She is hovering behind my eyes, her wet body sharp against the sky. Every time I turn my head and see the black glass of my office she is standing there, intense and staring. I do not like her, I am infected with her. She is a virus heating my skin. Nguyen's distaste is welcome, a cooling rag of reason.

She had no additional information to offer, merely restated that she spent five or six weeks — she is unsure of the dates — looking for Porter's body. When asked why she did this she replied that Cameron asked her to and then it just became something she had to do. She became obsessed with it. She claimed to have no prior knowledge of where the body might be, saying that if she had, she wouldn't have wasted all that time looking in the wrong places. She knows the river and its currents intimately and claimed it was impossible to tell where a body would turn up.

He got little more from the other river people. They keep to themselves. For some their main contact with the rest of humanity is Valentine's bread delivery. They had missed her while she was looking for Porter — some abused her at length. Porter and Jones were known on the river but not particularly liked. Hermits, the lot of them.

The weekend people were more forthcoming but had less to offer. They tended towards the "Ooh, aah, how exciting", type of response. They knew Valentine, "Wonderful bread and so colourful, you know". They did not know the old men.

The yellow folder holds background on the deceased. Orr has been busy. The computer age of policing, useful and abuseful. Ryan Porter was born in 1919 of Maisie Jane Porter (nee Gregson) and Frederick Ryan Porter in Double Bay. Maisie and Fred also had a son named Thomas (in honour of Maisie's father?) six years after Ryan. That appeared to be the limit of their issue. Family. A brother. Orr has been unable to find a record of his death, so I must assume that, despite Ted's claim, Thomas is still alive. And did Thomas sow the seed of his loins on fertile ground? Only just. He married Dorothy June Lupin in 1955 and had one child, Sean, a boy who was born ten years later.

Sean Porter is known to us. Two arrests for soliciting, both resulting in cautions, and one charge of possession of narcotics. He got three years and served eighteen months. Truth in sentencing. All this by the age of twenty-two. Last known address is three years ago. The address on his driver's licence is Double Bay. Probably Tom and Dot's place. I wonder if bad boy Sean has been to see Uncle Ryan lately.

Ryan Porter has never collected the pension or any social security benefit. He held a current driver's licence showing the river address. Orr has drawn a blank on his tax records. He doesn't appear to have any. Nor does Mr Edward Jones of Porters Creek.

Investments. Ted said that Ryan had made some investments. I make a note to send Orr off to the Securities Commission. If Porter invested in public companies he must be listed in somebody's share register.

Nguyen's face appears in the doorway.

"Sergeant Cameron just called, ma'am. She's got the *Annie Marie* down at the dry dock in Pyrmont, if you want to have a look at it. Physical Evidence is already there."

I hate driving in the rain. It's like being inside something dark and unknown. The horizon disappears to be replaced by half-seen images and faces that flash past the corners of your vision. The road surfaces are dark and treacherous with water, ominous with mayhem, shattered bodies and screaming brakes. I can always see the accidents, the crumpled cars in the sheen on the asphalt. I get up, stretch and toss Nguyen my keys.

"You can drive. The dock's under cover isn't it?"

He has the decency to hold his face still. They know I hate the wet roads.

It is still raining when we get to Harris Street. Typical city weather. It can rain like this for a fortnight then nothing but clear skies and high UV for months. Nguyen takes the car through the gates to the police wharf and pulls up next to a high black wall. The wall is the side of the dry dock. We run through the rain to a steel door and in to shelter.

The *Annie Marie* looks huge up out of the water. Cameron is standing a good twenty feet above us on the forward deck. She looks tired but happy. It is a long trip down the coast from the river, then up the harbour to here. She is coiling a thick white rope into a well in the deck. I stand and watch her as Nguyen trots off to harass two Physical Evidence officers who are studying the hull at the other end.

She seems to be happy with her temporary secondment to Homicide but it's early days yet. I need women sergeants. The number of female victims is disproportionately high and the number of women who decide the only way to get rid of an abusive partner is a quick whack on the head with a blunt instrument is growing. She would be an excellent replacement for Coburn. But one case is easy. Homicide can be dark and depressing. Mean petty deaths with no hope of an arrest. The constant shifting search for proof you know you're never going to find even when you're sure of the guilt. There aren't many cases with boats in them.

Finishing with her rope she clambers down a ladder leaning against the hull and comes over to me.

"How was the trip down?"

"Fine, ma'am. It was slow but the weather was okay. We got into the harbour before the squalls broke, thank heavens."

I nod toward the launch.

"Tell me about the boat?"

She reaches out her hand and gently pats the hull. It is red with anti-foul below the water line.

"Old Halversons like this are great boats, they just go on for ever. She's a big one too. Worth a bit. She's got satellite navigation gear, echo sounders, radar, long range tanks, the works. You could go around the world on her if you weren't in a hurry."

Her hand is still stroking the hull.

"She's very clean. They've had her up on the slip recently. There's hardly any growth on her at all. Usually a boat that sits on a mooring and doesn't go out much gets pretty fouled but this one's in very good nick."

"Cleaned recently? How recently?"

"Difficult to say exactly, but we scrape down the police boat every six months and a month after she's done there's some growth back again. There's a fair amount of enrichment in the river. It means the boats foul up pretty quickly."

We both gaze contemplatively at the smooth red surface in front of us. There isn't a barnacle or piece of seaweed to be seen on it. Cameron clears her throat and looks at me thoughtfully.

"Yes?"

"Well, I don't know, ma'am, but it doesn't seem to fit. I mean, that house and this boat. She's in near perfect condition. Inside is absolutely spotless. You could eat off the engine and yet they lived in that hovel as if they had nothing. But the *Annie Marie* must be worth nearly half a million with the gear she's carrying. It just seems such a contradiction."

"Have you never seen it before? Men who live in squalor but have a car or a motorbike they spend all their spare time polishing. It looks like Porter and Jones were boat freaks."

She grins.

"Yeah, but even so. The saloon and the staterooms are spotless, as if the cleaners have just been in."

"Maybe they have, sergeant."

I nod towards the other end of the dock.

"Tell Nguyen and the Physicals that I want their prelim report by morning. We'll have a briefing at eleven and I'll want you there."

She goes off and I turn back to the boat. It sits huge on its slipway. Full of possibilities. A boat you could go around the world in. A boat worth lots of money. A boat you could die on, perhaps.

I drive myself home. The rain has abated for the evening although the sky is still heavy with more to come. I live in a flat. There are six above it and six below, all identical in white brick, low ceilings and a tiny balcony offering glimpses of the city skyline to the south. It has little to commend it other than convenience. It is a short drive to work passing supermarket, newsagent and drycleaner on the way. The furniture is not mine. It came with the lease. I do little other than sleep here.

Like Valentine, I have few guests.

I am solitary by habit. I know that my life is my work. Homicide detectives are not socially desirable outside the force and inside — rank, ambition and sexuality have served to keep me separate. This has been an acceptable state of affairs.

It may sound barren but I have been content. Pleasure comes with the successful completion of the puzzle each case offers. I am pleased by a smooth, well-ordered department. And while I do not go out of my way to seek it, I enjoy the measured approval of those above me in the system.

And the needs of the flesh? I disregard them. There was a brief and painful liaison in the Academy but paranoia and anxiety drove her away. I have observed the violent and bloody results of too much passion too many times to feel the lack of it in my own life.

Until now. The surface of my smooth existence, measured in coloured folders and closed files, has been disrupted by a wild river girl. But there is power in habit so I will wrap my work and my method around me. I will armour myself with desk and keyboard and this fever will pass.

RIVER'S EDGE

PART TWO

Valentine

I have been slaughtering rabbits. Happily, an order for smoked bunny arrived at the same time as the deceaseds' maturity. It is not always so. But today there are eight pure white pelts drying on the shed wall and eight fat bodies slowly turning pink in the brine.

The order came from a new restaurant which has opened on the river. A new eatery, a place for the fashionable and the pretentious to strut and pose. Oh, joy. The chef is adventurous. He stepped into my path at the marina and engaged me in an intense and extended discussion. Well, intense on his part. He had heard about my bread. Lucky boy. I refused him that. I have no need of more baking. But bunnies, why not?

Hence this morning's labours. But I have deceived him. I will sell him these eight bunnies and no more. I have no desire to be "discovered" by the urban gourmands seeking new sensations to spark the jaded palate.

With luck the intense young chef will have six months' fame and then he and his patrons will find some more adventurous location and leave the river to those who understand it.

So, it's a taste of bunny for the new boy, a taste that will linger and entrance and never be repeated. Cruel, really.

I paddle afterward, after my morning's work is completed. It helps. It affirms the part I play in the flow of things. My animals are my friends and I thank them for their service. Slipping the kayak through the water is a cleansing, the completion of the process.

And a lovely day for a jaunt on the river it is too. A glorious blue and gold, gleaming-on-the-water day. There is no traffic, no other craft to break the surface. My lovely boat slides, smooth and slick through the water. I love this place, it flows and beats within me like my own blood.

I hear an engine and around the point comes an unwelcome intrusion. I recognise the boat but not the occupants. It is George's tinnie, yellow with a pink stripe across the bow. George cleans the slipway at the marina. He has no children but there are two boys in the boat. They are yelling and laughing, roaring in circles, bouncing over their own wake. Hoons. And thieves. The engine roars and falters, roars and falters. The boat surges back and forth across the channel. Boat thieves. I hate boat thieves. In particular adolescent boat thieves.

They have seen me. More sport. The boy at the tiller laughs and points for his buddy. They come straight for me. The bow gets closer. I can see the paint chipped and peeling. A dent marks the spot where George hit the wharf when he was drunk one night.

At the last moment the boy turns the boat and they roar around me. I bob in the wake, wet from the water splashed up by the prop.

Oh, they like this, this is fun. A captive, something to torture and frighten. They come back for more, the tinnie inches from my bow. The water is boiling, wake upon wake. Their laughter soars above the engine noise. A third pass. This is great sport.

I roll. I slip the paddle into the forward shock cords, tip my little boat over and stay upside down. I drop out of the seat and come back up inside, my head in the airspace in the cockpit, and hang there. I can stay here for a long time. There is plenty of air.

I can hear quite clearly through the skin of the kayak. The tinnie slows and stops. I can hear them talking. One is yelling at the other.

"Shit. Look what you've fucking done. Look. You've fucking drowned her!"

"Nah. No I haven't. She'll come up. They roll over in those things."

"You've fucking drowned her!"

There is nothing more enticing, more curiosity arousing than the upturned hull of a boat winking in the sunshine. They come in. Slowly, slowly. I can feel the wash from the prop around my legs. The boat's shadow comes closer. Very close, then stops.

"Come 'ere. Look, there's something down there. It's her body. You fucking drowned her! I told you!"

I dive and come straight back up in front of them. They are together, leaning over the gunwale. I grab a T-shirt in each hand and pull. Their own weight carries them over the side and into the water. I hold them under, a boy at the end of each stiff arm. They struggle, feet breaking the surface and kicking. Their heads stay down. I am very strong. I can hold them down like this for a very long time. As long as I wish, really.

One begins to weaken, his hands slipping around my wrist. The other tries to strike out and hit me but he can't reach. Stupid, they should be using their energy to conserve their breath. I wait a little longer, until the weaker one begins to go limp.

Up into the air and I smash them against the side of the tinnie. And what woeful, sputtering, blue-faced, pathetic little nothings they are.

They suck in air like it's their first breath.

I swim back to my kayak and flip it upright. The paddle float goes over the blade and I slither up across the rear deck, twist and slide back into the cockpit. As I sponge out the water, one boy manages to clamber back into the stolen tinnie. The other is still floundering.

I reset my spray skirt and paddle across to them. The one in the boat scrambles to the other side like I'm going to reach across and grab him again. Taking the floating one by the back of his T-shirt I hoist him out of the water and across my deck. He lies there in front of me, a rather peculiar shade of green. Leaning forward, I put my face very close to his.

"Take this boat back to where you got it and stay away from my river."

He slides back into the water and manages to flap away. His friend helps him as he flounders and flops back into George's boat. Stupid, dumb and violent. I hope they die in a car crash.

A wedge-tailed eagle has built a nest for herself on the railway bridge. She is alone. Her kind are rare here, our trees too close and the road kill too sparse. But for some reason she likes the bridge. It has seven soaring arches high above the water. She has nested on the top of the highest.

Her wingspan is over two metres and she flies with the primary feathers on her wingtips splayed wide. Black with tawny gold across her shoulders, she is the biggest bird in my sky.

When the trains plunge out of the tunnel and roar onto the bridge she rises up into the air crying at them. It is the main line north. There are trains every few minutes. She spends most of her time wheeling above her home moaning at the invaders below. She has no mate and her nest is ragged and badly built. Her strange choice of home is driving her mad, her cries as impotent against the trains as the river against the bridge.

I am hoeing in the lower beds. Peas out, sweet corn in. I put this corn in late to miss the storms and winds that can flatten a good crop in moments. The peas go in early to avoid the powdery mildew that dusts across every leaf at the first hint of summer humidity. Sometimes I get it right, sometimes I don't. The kookaburras follow me along the rows, diving for the worms I try not to leave exposed. They are a nasty and vicious bird, impervious to my threats and the occasional rock I throw at them.

While the image of a whistling kite soaring high in the blue can free my heart from despair, I don't actually like birds. Cold and sly things. The romance of the city dweller disappears like mud under the tide when you know the reality of bird land. There are wild ducks which live on my wharf. Last week the oldest pair hatched six ducklings. Yellow and tawny, their tiny little bodies paddle through the water every day. The kites dive out of the angophoras on the cliff and swoop on them. The parents leap up out of the water, four, five feet from nothing. Wings whirling, bodies twisted to protect their young. The kites seize the ducklings, break their backs then drop them in the water. They don't eat them, use them to feed their own young, or display any justification for the deaths. They just do it. Every year. Some babies survive, most don't. Bird land.

Stewart

Coburn is trying to make up lost ground. I see him in the outer office, avuncular, hail-fellow-well-met. He is talking to Cameron and Fargo. Fargo is one of my better inspectors. He has naked women tattooed on his forearms and an eagle on his left shoulder. Relics of a youth misspent exploring beer and motorcycles. But he is quick, almost as smart as Cameron. He usually has little time for Coburn but the sunshine seems to have infected them all with some kind of bonhomie.

The little group is joined by Jamie Orr. They should be working. We have far too many cases for time spent socialising in the office. Irritation distracts me from my own work. I tell myself to ignore them, fighting the urge to open my door and reproach them for wasting time. It's five-thirty on a sunny afternoon, be human. They don't know I am watching through the tinted glass. I pick up a new report and start reading.

When I raise my head again Fargo is looking at his watch and Coburn raises a glass in mime. Cameron shakes her head. The other three make encouraging gestures. She shrugs then glances towards my door. She tilts her head towards me and asks them something. There is a mixed reaction. Fargo laughs and shakes his head. Coburn's face goes flat and blank. Orr looks startled. Cameron spreads her hands wide, interrogative. Fargo is smiling and nodding.

While the others watch, Cameron clears her desk, picks up her bag and comes to my office. She knocks and enters.

"Some of us are just going to the pub, ma'am. Would you like to join us for a drink?"

"No thank you, sergeant."

"It's a lovely day, ma'am, we could just … I thought you might like …"

The blush rises up from her open collar, heating her face.

"Sorry, ma'am."

She rejoins the group and they walk toward the lifts. At the foyer door she hesitates a moment then follows.

Thomas and Dorothy June Porter live in a white apartment block three streets back from the Double Bay water. Two stories, two units on each floor. The building has been recently painted and a small well-kept garden lies between it and the street. The land of the Liberal voter and the upper middle class. Very respectable.

Thomas is anxious. So anxious he comes down to the foyer to meet me. He has difficulty with the stairs going back up and apologises all the way. He is elderly but, like his home, well kept. Hands manicured, hair trim, and clothes bought to last.

He has an air of capitulation about him, his rather handsome face undermined by weakness. Life has been more difficult than he expected and less rewarding.

Dorothy June meets us at the door to the unit. I shake her hand and she peers up at me, flustered.

"Hello, hello, Chief Inspector. I'm sorry, this is … oh, dear. Is it about Sean? Only we haven't seen him in a long while. I'm sorry … Tea, would you like a cup of tea? We … I don't think I've met a Chief Inspector before, not a woman one anyway, I'm sure. Thomas, dear, would you …?"

I seem to be rather more than she is used to. Thomas limps into the kitchen and starts to open cupboards. Dorothy June and I retire to the main room which has thick white carpet and white walls. The furniture is mahogany and chintz. Lladro figurines adorn the mantel of a gas fire. She keeps chattering to cover her confusion.

"We don't have very much to do with the police really. Well, there was that time when Sean had his little bit of trouble … You have come about Sean haven't you?"

Hope and fear battle for ascendancy in her bruised brown eyes. She has an attractive face, but like her husband's, worn down by disappointment.

"Why don't we wait for your husband? How long have you lived here?"

"Oh, years. This building used to belong to Thomas' father, you see. But we had to sell it. Thomas hasn't been all that successful … It's very hard, you know, competing with the young ones. Thomas always seemed to back the wrong schemes. Oh dear, you don't want to know about our troubles. Unless — do you? Is that why you're here? Has Thomas, has something … ?"

Thomas arrives at this point with tea cups on a tray and some pieces of homemade shortbread. After the fuss of serving he sits and they both wait.

"When was the last time you saw your brother Ryan, Mr Porter?"

"Ryan? You're here about Ryan? We don't see him. I haven't seen or heard from Ryan since just after the war. He didn't fight, you know. He just left. Up and left in that damn boat of his. No, I haven't seen Ryan since 1947."

"Why not?"

"I don't see what business it is … Oh well. We fought. We never did get on that well and he, well, today it doesn't seem to matter that much but back then."

"Did you fight about his homosexuality?"

"Not really. Although I suppose that was a part of it. I was angry, you see. I had spent most of my war in Egypt and he had just sailed away as though none of it mattered. I couldn't reconcile myself to that. It seemed to be the difference between us. I would do what was expected of me and he would just ignore convention. I knew that he had land up on the river but I never went there. It all seemed too much and then the years passed and somehow I was never able to … Has anything happened to him? Is that why you're here?"

"Well, yes, I'm sorry, but something has happened to him. He died about seven weeks ago under suspicious circumstances."

Thomas sighs and Dorothy June reaches across for his hand. She speaks first.

"What does that mean, suspicious circumstances? Does that mean that he was, oh, dear. Seven weeks ago? Why has it … Why have you come now?"

"His body has only just been found."

Pulling his hand away Thomas rubs his face. He sags in the chair.

"He had a friend. I don't know. I don't think I remember his name but there was someone he went away with. Maybe … is he … were they still … ?"

"His partner is Ted Jones. Mr Jones is still living on the river. They were together until Ryan's death."

"And did he … Did he kill Ryan?"

"Why would you think that?"

"Well, I don't know. I don't suppose I do really. It's just, who else is there?"

They try to take it in. The tea in the fine cups is ignored and goes cold. Dorothy starts to fidget until, unable to stay in her chair, she gets up and walks about the room, arthritic but still agile. She looks out the large windows to the bay.

"I always wondered, you know, about Sean. If Ryan's being like that had anything, whether … Well, they say it's genetic now, don't they."

The dear old soul is going just where I want her to.

"Did Sean know Ryan? I thought you said that you hadn't had any contact with him."

She turns back from the window and faces me across her sagging husband.

"No. No. Neither Sean nor I ever met Ryan. We knew, of course. Thomas told me and, well, when Sean was at school, he struggled, you know. With it. His sexuality. So I told him about Ryan, his uncle. Not about the war but that he was like that too. I thought maybe it would make things easier. It would help him, I don't know."

"Did Sean know Ryan's financial situation?"

Thomas lifts his head and comes back into play, his attention sharpened with resentment.

"He had the knack, you know. That's all it is, a knack. Hard work and dedication have nothing to do with it. Some people just make money. Ryan was always like that. It just came to him. Was he wealthy when he died? Of course he would be. Money doubled just sitting in his pockets."

"Did Sean know this, Mrs Porter?"

Turning his head to look back at his wife Thomas rises in his chair.

"Did you tell him that? Did you tell him that too?"

"Well, yes, dear, I may have done. I was trying to make him seem a good man, you know. Someone to look up to, someone Sean could admire. I didn't really know if he was wealthy or not, I just wanted to help Sean. To make it easier for him."

For a moment it's just between the two of them.

"Easier for him. That was the trouble. You were always making it easier for him."

He turns back to me.

"That's why you're here isn't it? You think Sean killed … You think Sean killed Ryan. Oh God, he has, hasn't he. That's what he's done. That's what my son has done. He's killed my brother."

"No, Thomas. How can you say that? He wouldn't. Sean isn't bad. How can you think that? It's wrong, Thomas. It's wrong to think so badly of him. Your son."

They meet between the chair and the window. She puts her hands on his shoulders and shakes him gently. He drops his head down to hers, his arms hanging.

"Mr Porter, we don't know who killed Ryan. At this point we have very little to go on. However, I would like to speak with Sean. Can you tell me where I can find him? His last official address is this one."

They both turn back to me and stand, side by side, holding hands. Dorothy June speaks for them.

"No, Chief Inspector. I'm sorry. We haven't heard from Sean for two years. He doesn't contact us and we don't know where he is. After he came out of, well, after his sentence ended, he didn't seem to want to know us. We were too different from what he had become used to. He became so hard. He would speak so harshly."

There are tears flowing down both faces.

"I'm sorry to have distressed you. The coroner has Ryan's body. If Mr Jones plans a service or anything I will ask him to let you know. I can let myself out."

But manners hold the world together. She follows me to the door.

"Please, Chief Inspector, if you see him — if you see Sean could you tell him, please … Tell him he can always come home."

I promise.

Valentine

It's a grey grey day. The hills roll back from the river in soft blue folds. Flat as a steel sheet, the grey-green water is pocked with the evanescent ripples of fat raindrops. Wet misty air hangs heavy over the world. Good garden weather. Good gentle growing rain. Tomorrow the pumpkins will have grown three feet.

I have a bad feeling, an itch, a disquiet, a worrying turbulence in the metaphysical. A portent. A slipping, sliding in the psyche. Something is wrong somewhere. Something near, something here, something that bothers me. Something that has drawn me away from my work and down to the wharf.

There's no answer in the river. The tide swirls inexorably past the poles of my wharf, just as it always does.

The dogs have it. They are looking north. Rosie's sister, Sharon, has her head up, straining forward. She whines, snaps at the dog by her shoulder, then whines some more. The others are troubled, twisting, pushing each other to get to the edge of the dock.

I shush them. Very faintly, a dog is barking in the distance.

Sharon is the only one I let in the tinnie and then we fly. The entrance to Porters Creek is shrouded in soft drizzle. Masked by the sound of my own engine, I don't hear the other boat until we are almost in the creek. It comes, very fast, from Ted and Ryan's.

It's white, fibreglass and new. Tunnel hull, no cabin and the controls in the centre. Three occupants. One standing up at the wheel but his face is obscured by the plexiglass windscreen in front of him. Two behind him standing amidships. They seem to be laughing. The skipper swerves to miss me and I thump, airborne, across his wake. He looks over his shoulder as he shoots by and I get a flash of white face, red hair. They are all definitely male.

The wash rebounds from side to side in the creek, ricocheting off the banks. I have to slow down as the tinnie slews dangerously. Around the bend and I can hear Rosie barking. Sharon starts up in reply.

There is smoke rising from the back of Ted's little blue house. Thick, dark smoke and it isn't coming out of the chimney. Sharon leaps from the boat as soon as we reach the jetty. I'm almost as fast but she gets up the hill before me.

Ted is lying face down just outside his back door. Rosie has him by the collar, tugging him away from the house between barks. Smoke is billowing from the kitchen door.

Inside the smoke is solid, dense and black. The fire seems to be coming from the floor in front of the woodstove. There is more smoke than flame. Above the stove there is a water tank balanced across two of the roof beams. Up on the table and I can reach one of the beams. I pull myself up and balance against the tank. The smoke is incredibly dense. It's almost impossible to breathe.

I can't see a thing but I can feel it. The tank is cool but I can't get a purchase. I turn, slipping on the beam, until my back's against the ridged metal side, wedging my feet against the next beam over. The smoke is so thick. Damn! I need to be able to breathe for this!

I feel it start to move. Just an inch. Then another. Then another. The water is slopping against the sides. The beam under my feet is bending. I try to get a decent lungful of air but there isn't any. And then it goes. I go with it. The tank crashes to the floor, water spilling through its ruptured sides. The beam scrapes the skin off my back as I follow it down.

The floor is spitting and hissing, hot steam burning my feet and legs. And more smoke, thicker and whiter. Out the door I collapse next to Ted. I never dreamed breathing could be so painful.

My eyes are streaming so I can't see him properly. I'm coughing so much I can't hold his pulse but his eyes are open and I think I hear him moan. Not easy, the dogs are still hysterical. Sharon is trying to climb on my back to lick my ears.

The air out here is good, moist and warm and I finally stop coughing. My eyes burn but I can't stop myself from rubbing them. The dogs shut up and the silence is as much relief as the clear atmosphere.

There is a nasty looking cut on the back of Ted's head. The blood has congealed in his hair, sticky dark red amongst the grimy grey. Apart from that he seems to be all right. He groans and rolls over onto his back, trying to sit up. Rosie hovers, more hindrance than help. Sharon sits on command, restless, bouncing on her front paws. The smoke from the house is clearing.

He doesn't look very pleased to see me.

"What the fuck is going on, Ted? Who did this? Who were those blokes in the fibreglass? Ted! Jesus Christ, you stupid old fuck. What the hell is going on?"

Right, Valentine. Really good way to handle someone in trauma. Yell at them.

"Sorry, Ted. I got a bit of a fright. I didn't mean to yell at you. What happened, mate?"

His bitten, tormented fingertips delicately explore the damaged part of his head. He grunts then inspects the blood on the ends of them.

"Don't know who they were. They just came in the back door and started calling me a filthy old poofter. Pushed me into the passage then hit me on the head."

"And that's all they said, that you're a filthy old poofter?"

"Yeah. Well, they threw in a few other things like, you know, scum and pervert and stuff."

"What about Rosie? What did she do?"

"Dunno. Barked a bit. I think they hit her with something. I heard her yelp when they were pushing me."

"How did they know about you and Ryan? Or did they know? Were they just a bunch of dickheads?"

"How do you expect me to bloody know?"

He's not happy with my interrogation so we both just sit there for a bit staring at the black doorway, now almost clear of smoke. After a while I get up and go back inside. The floor is still hot and my feet burn but I make it through to the two front rooms. It's impossible to tell if the redhead and his mates did anything in here or not, given Ted's housekeeping. There are filthy blankets tumbled across the bed and the other room is empty like it's always been.

In the kitchen the hardwood floor, although hot and blackened, did not burn through. Old rags piled up below the stove caused the smoke. The stove door is open and the firebox is empty, its hot embers raked out on to the rags. I kick them across the floor to where the water from the tank has pooled. They sizzle and spit then turn black.

Ted hasn't moved.

"It's not as bad as it looks but you'll need a new tank. You can come back with me for a couple of nights if you want."

But he doesn't want to. After grumbling and muttering about his broken tank, he gets up and walks, with surprising confidence, back into his smoky home. I stop Rosie from following him and run my hands over her. She winces when I touch her left shoulder. The muscle is beginning to swell. I go after Ted and tell him to use his hose and run cold water over her shoulder for half an hour morning and night. That should bring the swelling down. And that's it. Rosie stays with Ted and Sharon comes with me.

What is happening here? Where is all this viciousness and evil coming from?

Stewart

I enjoy our daily briefings, these meetings we have where the teams discuss the current cases. I find a tangible pleasure in the group workings. The minds together working in unison on the puzzle. In the time I have been here I have ensured that the minds, mostly, are good ones. The emotions and rivalries are kept to a minimum. We are serious people here working on serious crimes. The rest is rubbish, dross. You don't stay in my Homicide if you aren't concentrating on the task at hand.

There is one exception this morning. It is easier to watch someone who is working next to you than someone far away. I have changed my mind and asked Sergeant Coburn to join us. Orr and Nguyen are puzzled by this.

The files are spread out across the beige table. The table top is made from some kind of synthetic substance, pure public service, pleasingly nondescript.

Despite the cynicism common to all cops the faces around me are young and enthusiastic. These are the good ones. The new ones. Polished and refined. They want to crack this case. (Except Coburn, a life in parentheses.)

Not because they knew Porter or Jones but simply because it is a case, defined by the numbers and colours of the folders on the table top. Defined by the boundaries and limits of every investigation which has gone before and all that will follow. And Cameron because she likes boats.

The Physical Evidence report does not yet have a folder of its own so it sits, slightly forlorn, on the table, a slim sheaf of papers. And it raises more problems than it solves. The *Annie Marie* has been cleaned. She is absolutely spotless and carries her full complement of tools. A fifty millimetre spanner fits a particular nut on the cover of the starter motor but it too is clean. No human tissue or blood mars its surface. Three sets of fingerprints were on the boat — Porter's and Jones' are not among them. Nor are Sean's. None of the prints match any that are on file.

We sit in silence as we digest this. Caught by a slight movement, I look up to see Cameron.

"I think I may have the story on the boat, ma'am."

"Yes?"

She clears her throat, obviously pleased with herself.

"Well, on the weekend I did a bit of a trip around the main slips in the area. A boat that size, there are only a handful that can handle it. And we know it was out of the water because the hull's been done. So someone in the area must have either slipped her or seen it being done. Anyway, there was nothing in the local marina. They used to slip it a few years back but apparently they had a bit of a falling out with Porter over the quality of the work and the price so they don't do it anymore. They didn't know who did so I went further down the river. There are three slips at Pittwater big enough for it.

"It was the second one. Farley's Marine. They slipped her a couple of weeks ago. It's a standing order. Every six months they go up to Porters Creek and get the boat. They put her on the slip and clean the hull, service the engine and replace anything that's missing. They've been doing it now for five years. When they've finished they take the boat back and mail the bill. It always got paid within the week. They don't know Jones. Apparently they always dealt with Porter and nobody had told them he was dead. When I told him Farley was a bit worried about whether they would get paid this time."

Nguyen is in first.

"Didn't they try to make contact with Porter or see him when they went up the river to get the boat?"

"It seems that quite often they didn't see anybody. It was always done on the same date each time and when Porter made the original arrangements he said that he didn't want them coming to the house. Just to pick up the boat and then bring it back. They have their own set of keys. Oh, and the only thing missing this time was the fifty millimetre spanner that removes the cover on the starter motor. They replaced it."

Orr leans back in his chair and sighs.

"So. There's nothing on the boat because it gets a routine clean every six months. There might have been blood flowing in the scuppers but there's nothing for us because Porter was methodical."

Cameron comes back.

"I asked if there was anything unusual, anything they noticed but they didn't see a thing. The prints will be the workers at the slipway."

Nguyen is a lateral thinker. He keeps trying.

"Okay, if the slipway had a key to the boat what about someone there? Is there any connection to Porter other than as a client? If you know about the boat and you know the old man lives up there and you think he lives alone, why not pop up one day, bop him on the head and not worry about it because you know there isn't going to be any evidence."

My turn.

"Porter was killed nearly three months before the boat was cleaned. If you knew when the cleaning was going to take place why run the risk by killing him so early? Why not wait until a couple of days before and kill him then? We would find out about the slipway eventually and come looking for a connection."

Coburn needs to speak.

"What's it worth, a boat like that?"

This is Cameron's area and her face glows with enthusiasm.

"The *Annie Marie* is a beauty. She's loaded up with sat nav, radar, sounders, the works. Halversons are classic boats and she's been very well maintained. In today's market, maybe five hundred, five fifty."

"Half a million bucks! Where'd two old coots like that get that kind of money?"

Coburn is incredulous. In his presence Orr and Nguyen refuse to show surprise. I take control.

"I intend that we shall find out. Jamie, I want you back on the keyboard. Keep searching the Securities Commission. There must be something somewhere that indicates what their investments are. Check with Cameron's marina and find out how the bill was paid. If it was by a company cheque then follow up the company. It's still far too early in this case to go looking for easy solutions. So far it would seem there is some missing family and a definite mystery in the money area. The two old reliables.

"Cameron, get back to the marina and take the prints of the people who worked on the boat. We may as well get that out of the way. Nguyen, you go with her and poke around a bit. See if there's any kind of link between the marina and Sean Porter. It would be nice and easy if there was but I wouldn't bet on it. It would be nice to know if Sean knows how to handle a boat like that.

"Coburn, I want you to find Sean Porter. I don't want you to talk to him or have any contact with him at all. Just find out where he is and what his days and nights consist of. Don't spook him."

This order is not so strange. Coburn is a good street cop if somewhat heavy handed. He should be able to pull this one off. He spent five years on the beat in Darlinghurst. Conflicting emotions play on his broad pink face. He's thankful that I'm using him, that's he's in on the job, but he's wondering why.

Nguyen is bothered by Valentine. He distrusts and suspects her but is too professional to assume she is the killer just because he doesn't like her.

"We have to get more out of Jones and Valentine. I reckon they hold the keys to this."

"I agree with you, Sam, but the direct approach doesn't really work with either of them. I'll handle that part of it. Alice, can you arrange for me to have a small boat that I can use myself? Something discreet and easy. I think I'd like to go fishing."

She grins back at me. I stand up and gather the coloured folders, tapping them even on the table top. The meeting is over.

He wants something from me but he doesn't know how to get it out. Hope and fear are running ragged behind his wet old eyes. Ted is healthy again but the brief sojourn on the island did not encourage him to change his personal habits. He is filthy and smells like burnt humus. So do I. We have been putting in his new water tank.

He seems to have no interest in his assailants or the reasons for the attack despite his flirt with the reaper. Ted is distracted, his mind on something else and, unusually, he came back with me for refreshments. Now I know why he did. His hands are grimy and wrapped around a mug of tea.

He has corruption in his gaze. Rotten and diseased. He is caught between what he wants and what he fears. Desire and repulsion. He puts the tea down and picks at his fingers. A bad sign. It is a miracle that his nails are still there. I keep expecting to see bleeding stumps pulling blindly at their own flesh. Poor Ted. Poor aching bleeding Ted.

"I need you to help me."

"What with?"

He ducks his head, his right shoulder coming up to meet his ear. His eyes slither around the table for a bit and then something happens. A shift occurs, a change inside him. The yellowed eyes are staring straight at me. The pain has been moved aside.

"I know who did it … I know who did it and I need you to help me get them."

The air goes sharp and still. Even the dogs are still. A deep wrinkle bisects the side of his cheek just to the left of his nose. It is dark with dirt, a valley lined with grey stubble. This crevice in his face takes all my attention. I cannot look away from it.

He knows who did it. For a millisecond I think he means the fire but then I remember that he doesn't care about that.

Then suddenly the words come tumbling out of him, a tumbling rolling torrent.

"There's a nephew. Ryan had a nephew. He came up here. I didn't tell the cops. I won't ever tell the cops. He came here to see Ryan the day he went missing. He wrote a letter asking for money and saying he was going to come. The nephew — he killed Ryan. He knew about the money. Me and Ryan. We've got money and the nephew knew. That's why he came. They took the boat. That's where it happened, on the boat. I knew, see. When I realised the diesel had gone down. They took the boat out and killed him. But I need you to help me."

So that's what's been eating your poor little heart out — knowledge of a deed so foul. And now you want to act. You have to share your secret because now you want to do something about it. But don't tell the coppers. Don't tell those cold-eyed people in their pretty blue uniforms. Don't tell my lovely girl with the grey eyes and the quiet smile. Just tell me and ask for my help. Who else is the poor old bastard going to ask? Who else does he know?

Ryan had a nephew and that nephew killed him. For money, Ted says. Money? How much money? Lots of money? Were my two old hermit friends misers, perhaps? I never really thought about it, their money. A killing for cash. Most foul indeed.

One secret leads to another. What are we going to do with this nephew when we find him, Ted, dear? Do I have to ask or are you going to tell me?

"I have to find him. He has a friend. Ryan said that he was coming to see him with a friend. There are two of them. I know he lives in the city. The gay part. He hangs around the gay ghetto. Ryan said he was a rent boy."

He wants to punish. I can see it in the grasping of his hands, in the catching of his breath, the glitter of those old eyes now focused and sharp. He wants to punish. My morose old friend thinks punishment will make him feel better.

"I've got his address. It was on the letter."

The catching, judging and punishment of those who killed his love will make the pain and loneliness lose its edge. He will have restored Ryan in the punishing of his killers. This ravaged old man sitting in my kitchen is planning murder and mayhem.

He wants me to help.

"What do we do when we find this nephew and his friend, Ted?"

"They killed Ryan. They have to pay for that, Valentine. They have to pay."

There is no question for him of telling the cops, handing it over. Of giving up the desire, the need to exact vengeance. He wants to see their bodies turning through the water like Ryan's did. He wants their heads smashed like Ryan's was. He wants them to know they are going to die for the deed they did to an old man on a boat in the middle of my river.

A killing. Ted wants me to help him with his killing. He wants me to help him with the housekeeping of his emotions.

I get up and walk outside to the sunshine. Most of the dogs scramble up and follow. The gardens are sparkling and pristine in the clear light. I have been harvesting seaweed and a large pile of dark brown kelp glistens by the compost bins. In the bright light with my work laid out before me, I consider dear Ted's request.

Do I fear killing? Is killing a man somehow different? A man can say, "Let me live." A man can plead where a pig cannot. I live with animals, I raise my animals, they are mine and I am theirs. My pig is my friend and I hear the voices of my friends. I feel the sharp sting when the blade slices across the throat. My debt to them is far greater than that to any man. I can kill because I know it. I can kill because I am strong.

But is this a killing I desire? Is this an action that I must take? Ted's need is easy and terrible to see. Mine? The loss I feel from Ryan's death is of a different nature. He was my friend not my love. I miss him but there is no hollow place in me where the wind rushes through.

And my time on the river, the search for that bloated pile of decay? Was that for him or me? Or the river? Is everything in my life now guided and determined by the water I can see flowing below me?

This will need some thinking about. I have work to do, a routine to follow. Ted's howling heart will have to wait until the chores are done.

I go back inside. He is still sitting at the table. The face he turns towards me is both desperate with hope and doomed with resignation. I tell him I need to think about it. Behind the quick anger he is resigned.

Stewart

I report to my boss thrice weekly. Superintendent Ray Matthews, Commander of the Regional Crime Squad.

Matthews is not bad. What he lacks in imagination he makes up for with caution and due diligence. A hard worker and as far as I can make out, honest. We meet three times a week usually, unless there is one of those cases that excite the media and inflame the politicians.

Today he is in uniform. White shirt starched and pressed, crowns gleaming on his shoulders. I can smell his shaving lotion and his cheeks are freshly pink. There is a special meeting called at College Street this afternoon. His boss, Assistant Commissioner Peter Slade, Northern Regional Commander, is meeting with his peers and the Minister and he wants Matthews there for back up. Parliament has been talking about corruption again.

Our briefings are far more mundane.

"How goes it, Jane? What have you got today? You know, Mick Coburn was telling me yesterday that this Porter case on the river is pretty much done. He says this Valentine woman is looking pretty good for it."

"Yesterday was Sunday. I didn't know you were close with Coburn."

"Oh, well, I'm not really. He's not a friend of mine, you know. My daughter, she goes to uni with his wife. They're good friends. Christine had the Coburns over for a bit of dinner last night. I wasn't really there, didn't get in from the club until late. Mick was just bending my ear for a bit before they left."

"He's wrong. And he is playing a very minor role in this case. Most of the people involved are gay, and sensitivity is not Coburn's strong suit. Valentine is a major witness but there is nothing, at this point, to indicate her involvement in the killing."

I hand him the Godfrey Reports, one page summaries of progress on all the current cases. He shuffles them around a bit. He has something on his mind and is having trouble getting it off.

"This … um … this gay thing. It wouldn't be creating a problem for you, would it, Jane? I mean, I don't want to know about your personal life or anything like that, of course, but you wouldn't … What am I trying to say here? You are maintaining a distance aren't you? Of course you are, you're one of the best we've ever had. I don't mean that. It's just something Mick said last night. Not that I would give it any weight of course but you know how these things are."

"Sir?"

I've never seen him floundering like this before. His eyes are firmly fixed to the pages on the desk before him and his right hand is tapping a tattoo on the wood. I concentrate on his embarrassment and try to disregard the small worm squirming in my gut.

"Look, I'm sure there is nothing ... You would have to be the most conscientious and dedicated officer I've ever had the pleasure of working with. Forget it. Coburn was just being sly. He's a bit like that, Jane. You should keep an eye on him."

"What did he say to you?"

"Oh, well, I wouldn't want to repeat it, you know. But I'm sure he was just trying to cause trouble. Some of them resent it, you know. Your success and methods. Being a woman of course. Well, I don't have to tell you."

"If Coburn raised a concern about this case and my leadership, however informally, then I think that I should know what it is."

"Yes, yes, of course, you're quite right. He said that he believed it possible that you may, ah, become, uhm, distracted by this Valentine woman and the fact that, as you just said, most of those involved in this Porter case are gay. But I have to say, Jane, that I have seen no evidence of this and I have every confidence that you will bring to this case the diligence and care that you bring to all of your work. Yes, I have every confidence in you."

My intestines cramp and a sharp pain slides through me. I hold absolutely still and wait for it to pass. My silence brings his eyes up and he tries a smile. I slowly count a breath in and a breath out. The pain diminishes and the cramp recedes.

"If I thought there was a problem I would ask you to oversee my involvement in this case. I have been keeping an eye on Mick for some time. His record is less than spotless."

"Yes, yes, of course. Well, I'm running a bit late so if you don't mind, I'll have to get on. Thanks for these and I'll see you again on Wednesday."

"Sir."

We push our chairs out and stand at the same time. He looks relieved. My abdomen is in turmoil. I go straight to the bathroom.

Cameron and Coburn are arguing. He is a good four inches taller than she is and exploiting it. Belly and shoulders belligerent. She is standing taut, refusing to surrender, knees flexed.

They are leaning towards each other too intent on what they are saying to notice me. I have just come up the fire stairs to our floor. They are in front of the lift.

Coburn makes an obscene gesture with his hands, plunging two fingers of his right into the circle of his left. Cameron goes pale and looks as if she is about to hit him.

The lift bell distracts him and he turns his head. And sees me. He stops talking and steps back from Cameron. She turns as the lift doors open and steps inside. I can see her face in the lift mirror — white and tense. He steps in behind her.

The doors close.

Valentine

I haven't been looking for it. There has been no mad search this time. This time I just waited. I knew it would come. One day I would see it and know it. And now it sits, here, just in front of my bow, washed with the late afternoon sunlight.

White fibreglass, tunnel hull, central console with plexiglass windscreen, fifty horse on the back. It's tied up outside Old Beau Brumby's place. Beau's been dead for years and it looks like his daughter has finally found some renters. The house is pale green fibro, plain, with a rotting verandah about to drop past the sandstone drywall and into the mud.

The jetty has been repaired. Two new hardwood piles support yellow gum stringers and planking. The tops of the piles have been freshly painted white. The white boat is on a running line swung into the racing tide where it bounces and bobs.

Always good to welcome new folks to the area. The door falls open as I knock on it. The front of the house is one large room dominated by a brand new wide screen TV perched on its own packing case. A couple of dirty brown sofas face it, a garbage bin loaded with crushed beer cans is an occasional table between them.

The kitchen offers evidence of a modern lifestyle and more than one occupant. Fast food containers and pizza cartons decorate the benches and a table held up with milk crates. The decorations are as discriminating as the cuisine.

Out the back, bare dirt has been beaten down by the nervous paws of a brindled pitbull. He is chained to a wire clothesline, straining against its restraint. He's growling and yipping, lunging into the air.

But it's fear. When I move towards him, low so I'm no threat, he leaps back, flinching away from me. A big framed dog, he's thin, his coat patchy between his scarred shoulders and above his docked tail.

Oh, hollow men, oh, empty and thin abusers of the innocent, jailers of the free. To take a dog and starve him, to take a dog and parch him, to chain him and tie him shows nothing but the vacuum of your soul. The abuse of animals, the casual indifference to suffering and pain, the deliberate torture for pleasure and profit is the debasement of humanity. Evil and empty. These are not river dwellers, these are invaders, violaters of the water and air.

Back in the kitchen I find a plastic ice cream container and a couple of ancient slices of pizza, crusted and dry, left inside one of the boxes.

While he's distracted with the food I put the water where he can reach it.

Little piles of dog shit dot the yard going white and hard in the sun. A small grove of pittosporums is divided by a dirt road that turns and runs into the blackbutts under the cliffs.

As the dog tries to drink more than he probably should I unclip his chain from the clothesline. At first he's so busy drinking he barely notices. When he realises that ownership has just been transferred he flinches away from me, ears back and lip curled.

Dropping down into the dirt beside him I just sit for a bit. It takes a few minutes but eventually he stops snarling long enough to sniff my toes. Come on Dog, I'm on your side and I'm probably the best bet you've ever had. Not all humans are testosterone drenched lumps of dung. When I put my hand out, low down, palm up, he lets me touch him. The hair comes off as I rub him behind his ears.

We both hear the rumble of tires on gravel and a rusted calf-shit yellow Landcruiser rolls into the yard. Dog drops down and hides behind me. There are four occupants, three male, one female, and they don't look pleased to see me. The driver is the redhead but he's the last one out. The other two men both carry a couple of slabs of VB each. The woman, as befits her role, is clutching boxes of Kentucky Fried. Obviously a trip to the health food store.

The men are only about average height, unshaven, nondescript. But there are three of them. Father, Son and Holy Ghost. The trinity of evil. Dog beaters. With whore in tow.

"Hi. I've just come to get the dog."

The first two look at each other, register that I'm female and hence of possible sexual interest and absolutely no threat. The redhead glances at the dog then back at me, hostile.

The tallest one, loose jeans, T-shirt adorned with a leaping marlin, doesn't think this is a very good idea.

"What are you talking about? Who the fuck are you? What do you mean, take the dog? You can't have that dog. He's a fighter."

Standing up I'm taller than all of them and I catch the surprise on Red's face. Marlin recognises me.

"Shit, you're that bitch from down the river. The one we saw."

It takes a moment but he looks a tad chagrined when he realises what he's just said.

"Oh, shit."

He turns to Red for some support.

"We can't just let her take the dog, mate. What about next week? The fight?"

Number Three puts his slabs on the ground and comes towards my on my right flank. I lift my singlet off my hip exposing my knife. He pauses then steps back.

"I think this dog would like a new home. He's coming with me, isn't he, Red?"

The dog agrees, pushing against my legs. Heads flick from me to Red and back again. Red takes a couple of steps forward and Marlin follows. I shift my feet a little further apart to get my balance, then lean forward, just a little.

"You know, fibreglass boats tend to stand out a bit on the river. Not many locals have them. They don't stand up to the rocks and the foul in the water too well."

The sun seems to be hotter now than it was when I first got here. Red's freckled skin is flushed and he's having trouble with his hands. They clench and tremble by his thighs.

The hate and the fear that sent him up the river to Ted are bubbling inside. But they do him no good. Futility can drive us all crazy but you need a bit more than just bitter resentment to act. His eyes are light brown, tawny with gold flecks, freckled lines radiating out from the corners. I can see the thoughts scrolling behind them. This walking vacuum beats up on old poofters and brutalises animals. Whatever his rotten veins are awash with it isn't going to be courage.

My hands begin to tingle. I want to hit him.These men beat Ted and left him lying unconscious in his burning house. I want to hit this skinny little nothing. I want to beat and batter the lot of them, the woman included. Thump their brains out against a rock. My fists have clenched of their own accord and I'm bouncing on the balls of my feet. Red takes a step back and the others are defeated with him.

"Cunt."

That's all he can manage so Dog and I turn and walk away down the side of the house, Dog nearly knocking me over in a bid to get in front and escape. No one follows. I hear them walk inside, the walls trembling with their footsteps, low voices whining.

Dog is too frightened to get in the tinnie. Boats don't appear to hold much comfort for him so I pick him up and carry him in. Red and his family have come out onto the verandah, watching. Marlin yells something but I can't hear it in the roar of my engine. But I understand the gesture as a full can of beer comes hurtling towards me. It falls short and rolls off the dock. I don't take it as an invitation to stay.

Trash. They would have put up some kind of fight if they cared about the dog. Or had any guts.

Stewart

The river is bewildering. Cameron has found a small aluminium dinghy with a ten horsepower motor. It looks as though it has seen better days but she assures me it runs and won't sink. I get a quick lesson in forwards and backwards and am left to my own devices.

This is no gentle stream running quietly to the sea. It is a giant, massive waterway pouring between huge red cliffs. Endless bays and coves run back into the hills, twisting and turning upon themselves.

It is impossible to speak of the river bank. There isn't one, there are many. Covered in scrub and bush. Giant trees up on the cliff tops, mangroves and smaller shrubs down on the lower slopes. And mud.

The tide recedes leaving vast flats of dark brown goop which ooze and suck at the foot. And behind the mud, rocks lie pocked and jumbled. Sharp with old oyster shells and slippery with weed.

This is Valentine's world. And Ryan Porter's. I am losing sight of the dead man in the glow from the living woman. Porter has lived here most of his life. He must have been as familiar as she with the river and its nooks and crannies.

Why would he come out of his creek, his protection, in that big launch? And where would he go? Someone went with him. Someone who brought the launch back, locked it up and then left. In another boat. The boat that he or she must have come in.

And who would have seen them? Almost no other traffic moves on the water today. It is mid-week. I have seen two big barges in what I think are oyster farms and a commercial fisherman. All people Nguyen would already have spoken to.

According to Jones no visitors were expected. So whoever they were, they must have surprised him. And persuaded him to take the launch out. For a day on the water, fishing, a picnic? Porter and Jones do not seem the picnicking kind.

Or a nephew who needs money and decides to pay a visit to a vulnerable old man. Planned or opportunistic? Does he pester his uncle until the man gives in and off they go for a boat trip and a chat? A chat that goes wrong?

No answers to that one until Coburn finds Sean Porter. In the meantime, I putter between cliffs and try to make some sense of the geography. I should be in the office. I have no shortage of work. This is an indulgence, to be out here in the spring sunshine, messing about in a boat, trying not to think about the depth of the water. This is not an important case and the stack of reports on my desk grows. Here I sit watching the fish jump out of the water and the sunlight flash from the waves. Pretending that the river will bring me closer to Valentine.

"The Coroner wants to release Porter's body, Mr Jones. This means someone has to make arrangements for its disposal. It is usually the next of kin. In view of your relationship with Porter I presume that is you, yes?"

He is sitting on an old kitchen chair, the seat torn and faded, legs rusted and sinking into the garden soil. Face turned away, he has yet to acknowledge my presence.

"Mr Jones, you can have Porter's body or I can contact his brother. It's up to you."

That gets his attention.

"He doesn't have a brother."

"Mr Jones. The state keeps comprehensive records of births and deaths as I am sure you know. I know exactly how many Porters there are. Now either you do something with the body or someone else will. Do you want it?"

Dropping the weeding fork into a broken bucket beside him, he rolls his head back on his neck. He gazes straight up into the sky, face as blank as an idiot's.

"There has been a fire here. I can smell it. What happened?"

There's nothing, no reply. Looking back at the house the kitchen door is blackened and the interior seems darker and dirtier than usual. But he's not going to tell me.

"Go away."

As I walk back to Cameron's little boat I think about charging him with obstruction. But it's only a passing thought. What good would it do? Even if he does have the answers, he still wouldn't share them. We mean nothing to him.

Valentine

Dog isn't doing too well. Brutality does not help a dog develop. He is only a couple of years old but his social skills are nonexistent. The other dogs make him nervous and there have been a number of scraps. He attacks out of fear and, because of his poor debased breed, he doesn't know when to stop.

Sharon has a nasty rip in her right shoulder and a couple of the others are also bearing the scars of his outrageous fortune. What to do. I've knackered him. Breeding from a pit bull is the last thing I want, handsome though he is. It hasn't helped.

My happy, goodnatured-until-you-cross-them pack has become a skittish group of anxious biters. What to do. He competes aggressively for my attention, snapping and driving his rivals out of the way.

He looks better, filled out with glowing coat, polished mahogany shoulders rippling with muscle and grey-black brindle stripes. The mange is gone and the scars hidden. Understandably, he's obsessed with food and I have to tie him at feeding time or he steals.

But worst of all, he won't learn. Red's beaten him so much he can't think anymore. Fighting is the only thing he seems to know. If it was just him, if there were no others, if I had no responsibilities but him, then perhaps he would have a chance.

He's had the cow in a lather of terror, eyes rolling, sides flecked with foam and heaving like she'd just run the Melbourne Cup. Jersey cows are sensitive and delicate creatures, trusting and kind. It will be a long time before she recovers from such an ordeal. The pig escaped harm only because she fought him off from the sty door long enough for me to get there. Worst of all, he ripped the throat out of a kid, dragging her tiny body, entrails bloody in the dust, up to the house. He is a killer.

We are a small and well run community here, my friends and I. A community which this poor tortured creature is destroying.

What to do. I know what to do but before I do it a very large and angry part of me wants someone else to suffer first. Someone with two legs. When I look at this poor demented dog I roil and boil. The nasty small viciousness of it all. How dare he bring his empty redheaded soul and his mindless minions here to my river?

What to do. I will purge myself of this anger. When I deal with Dog we must both be at peace.

The tinnie. I need the cleansing power of speed. The afternoon westerly has picked up, pushing the water into a sharp chop. The boat bangs across the waves, flying from one crest to another, bow in the air, the stern crashing down so hard my brain aches. I am forced to slow down which does not improve my mood.

I cannot accept cruelty. More than any other vile human aberration it drives me to action.

An old banana grove persists in the midst of the eucalypts about five hundred metres east of Old Beau's. Many times I have told myself to give the plants some attention and see if they fruit properly. A bit of mulch, a little compost and they will probably be marvels. But not today. Today I'm busy.

The sagging green fibro is caught in the sun's glow and all its world is painted gold. But the white fibreglass is gone. The front door is locked and when I peer through the dust and the sunlight on the windows the TV has gone.

There's no Landcruiser out the back. Dog's clothesline remains, keeping company with a pile of orange garbage bags that give a beercan clank when I kick them.

Oh, frustration and bother, the vicious little gang has run. Gone, gone to some other place to leave some other old man to die in the smoke of his own home, to torture some other dog.

Red will get drunk in some sweaty pub one night, have a fight and get kicked severely in the head. Then he'll be a paraplegic and some stupid journalist will write a feature about the tragic destruction of his young life. His parents will blame the publican, the hospital, the social services, anyone but themselves.

All this anger and rage and nowhere to vent it. I must compose myself. I have a duty to Dog.

That evening I leave the others behind and take Dog up to the angophoras on the cliff. We sit watching the sunset brand the sky with flame, burning clouds climbing the horizon with the dropping of the westerly. The trains roar across the bridge far below us in the distance and each time I can see the wedge-tailed eagle rise up and cry.

Dog cuddles close, pleased to be the only one. My arm's around him. I rub his fine ears and tell him he's a bold dog. I tell him I'm sorry and it isn't his fault. I put the .22 to his head and kill him.

Stewart

"There's been another killing down on the river, ma'am."

The voice is Cameron's, the office mine.

"A woman named Sandy Masterson appears to have been killed by her husband. There's a history of domestics. I know them both. He's a drunken lout with a bad temper. Anyway, she's dead. Hornsby are down there at the moment."

"Do you want to go and have a look?"

"I think so. I don't think there's any connection with the Porter case, though. This is a straightforward domestic."

She looks depressed. I wonder how well she knew Sandy Masterson.

"Get a car out. I'll come with you."

"Yes, ma'am."

Another death on the river. Nothing for years and then suddenly, bang, they start killing each other.

Wildflowers line the sides of the freeway as we drive down the hill. Delicate spots of colour in the dry prickly grey of the bush. Cameron is tense, hands placed with regulation correctness on the wheel.

"Masterson has a boat. Ugly big black thing called *Bulletproof*. He claims to race it but I don't think he does. I've never seen it in the water, it just sits there on the trailer. Like most of those wankers. He's probably too scared to drive it."

"Is there something particularly scary about that kind of boat?"

"They are very, very fast. Men like Masterson see them racing on the telly and think they'd like to do it too. So, they go out and buy some overpowered thing and they have no experience. They load up their mates and a few beers, go out and open it up. The first corner they come to scares them so much they never take it back in the water. But their dicks are involved so they can't admit it. The boat just sits on the trailer in the front yard. A testimony to machismo."

She gives me a quick look and then grins.

"I would like to stay in Homicide, ma'am. I am enjoying it. The focus, not being distracted by all the petty rubbish that goes on in a patrol. Would it be possible for me to stay on after the Porter case is finished?"

"I already have two sergeants. I would have to plead a very good case to have three."

"Ma'am."

"What about Coburn?"

"Ma'am?"

"Come on Alice, I've seen you fighting with him."

"Coburn's attitudes towards ... well, anyone not strictly white and nuclear family ... are different from mine. But I can work with him, ma'am. I've seen worse on the job."

"I'll see what I can do. Maybe one of the others is thinking of a transfer."

"Thank you, ma'am."

I already plan to have her secondment made permanent. But she doesn't need to think it's that easy.

She almost misses the turnoff.

A couple of patrol cars and an unmarked are parked outside a small neat fibro house. The garden is plain but the lawns are mown and weed-free.

We walk up a wide concrete drive which runs up the side of the house to a carport at the back of the section. A big flat black boat with an enormous engine in the middle and a sharp nose sits on a trailer on the lawn. The trailer tyres are flat and the grass has grown around them.

Behind the backyard, scrubby bush rises up the hillside to an embankment carrying the railway line. The house is sandwiched between road and railway. Not even a water view. The trees on the other side of the road block that.

A concrete pad extends out from the back of the house. Someone has marked it off with police tape. These few square metres now belong to us for as long as we want them. Three uniforms are standing, bored, hands in their pockets, contemplating the scene.

The place stinks of beer. Inside the tape a plastic and aluminium chair has fallen on its side. Pieces of the plastic webbing are broken and stretched. It wouldn't fetch fifty cents at a garage sale. Beside it is an oversize plastic bucket. It looks as if it would hold about twenty litres and has been knocked over. Its contents have flooded the concrete. Thick brown residue has pooled on the inside of the bucket and slowly oozes over the lip.

The fermenting beer has attracted a swarm of tiny fruit flies. A small cloud hovers above the liquid, the bodies of the more adventurous insects floating on the surface.

Three blow-flies buzz by the bucket. They are attracted by Sandy Masterson. She is lying, blue, face down and small. A cotton print dress is rucked up around her thighs. Fresh grazes and abrasions mark her knees and elbows. She has long light brown hair which has come loose from its tie. Her head is soaking wet. She is an island in a shallow amber lake. The flies keep landing on her broken skin then taking off again.

A big man in jeans and windbreaker steps across the tape to Cameron.

"Gidday, Alice. Looks like the bastard finally did it. He drowned her in his home brew. Must have held her down in it for a good five minutes. He just sat in the chair and held her head in the bucket until she stopped kicking. Says she was nagging him."

Cameron turns her head towards me.

"Ma'am, this is DS Turnbull. From Hornsby. Dennis, DCI Stewart, Homicide."

Turnbull gives me a look.

"Is Homicide going to be taking this case then, ma'am?"

"I don't know yet, sergeant. Where's Masterson?"

"He's inside. He's pretty drunk."

I follow Cameron through the back door and into a good-sized kitchen. She has a somewhat proprietorial air, familiar with the place and its inhabitants. A huge man is sitting at the table, splayed back in a wooden kitchen chair as if his body is too heavy to hold up. He is pink and white. Ginger hair and beard, hasn't shaved for a couple of weeks, freckles scattered across a skin that is pallid, tinged with grey under the beer flush.

His belly protrudes out and pushes against the table. The table edge makes him look as if he is cut in half. A lime-green T-shirt barely holds all that flesh together. How did that tiny woman lying out there on the concrete find anything to love in this booze-soaked mountain?

He is justifying himself to the detective sitting opposite. Belligerent and aggressive.

"Fucking bitch just kept nagging. Wouldn't fucking shut up. I fucking whacked her but she still wouldn't shut up. Whingeing on and on all the bloody time. Jesus. It'd drive anybody nuts. You try livin' with that. Christ. It wasn't my bloody fault if she couldn't hold her fucking breath, was it? Stupid bitch."

Why did I come here? I hate domestics. We don't need this case. Hornsby can have it.

I go back outside to the wet and broken body of his wife. She must have been in her late twenties. What a life. There is nothing to say, nothing to think. It is all so humdrum, so ordinary and common. It will probably make the evening news if only for the home brew. Then disappear. Just another domestic. Of course, if it was him lying there on the concrete and her inside talking then things would be different.

Cameron comes up behind me.

"Dennis wants to know if we're going to take the case over, ma'am. He wants to get Masterson up to the station."

"It's all his, Alice. We don't need this."

She turns back into the house and I walk down the drive towards the car. The trees across the road are mangroves and the scent of mud wafts across. I can still smell the beer on the warm concrete.

Cameron comes down behind me. I hear her steps. I turn away from the car and look back. Valentine is standing on the railway embankment looking towards the back of the house. Her singlet catches the light. We both hear it at the same time. A solid roar of noise. The train bursts out from the cutting behind her and she turns away into the bush. Gone.

RIVER'S EDGE

PART THREE

Valentine

Rage and anger. That's all I've got. I stand here on this hillside shaking. A fever of fury. To kill her like that, casual, offhand, as if she were nothing more than a piece of refuse for the dump.

How can these people be like this? Here, on the shores of my river. How can they live so shallow, so narrow, so evil? These burners and beaters, boat thieves and killers. This fury bubbles and rolls within me. Who brought these people here? Who allows this? This easy destruction, this splashing in the shallows of contempt.

I hate these empty men, these empty useless drunken men. These choristers who wail a song of diminished responsibility.

"The drink made me do it, your honour."

"Society made me do it, your honour."

"It wasn't my fault, your honour."

"I didn't know what I was doing, your honour."

"She nagged me, your honour."

"He was just a poofter, your honour."

And the bench of yet more empty men hear their song and hum the tune.

"Poor chap. She was such a nag, slut, bitch, whore. Of course, one can't condone but even so. There have been times when I've thought myself, well, you know … "

The poor little bitch tried so hard, convinced that every fist in the face was deserved because he told her so. He hit her and smacked her and hit her and smacked her until she no longer existed. Until she was only what he said she was. Nothing.

He said it so often that he believed it too. What did he kill? Nothing. Just a wife. But, no, he didn't *kill* her. How can you kill nothing? He just made her quiet. Shut her up so he wouldn't have to listen anymore. Vile and filthy creature, bloated toad.

She was just two breasts and a cunt, something killable, something soft that thuds against a wall. Something weak you can hold in a bucket of beer until she makes no more sound, no more movement.

And for this will he be punished? Don't make me laugh. A slap on his wrist. And the plaudits, the praise of sycophantic cellmates, impressed by his size and capacity for alcohol.

"What are you in for, mate?"

"Drowned me missus in a bucket of beer."

"Never! Ya what? Bit of a waste of brew, eh."

A pat on the back and the admiration of the like. Dumb, incarcerated cripples. Men who sit, a row of empty bottles, their only function to fill up with beer.

I brew beer. I make my own. Beer is the sister of bread. One of the family of yeast, a part of the glory of ferment. He has despoiled it, he has desecrated the craft.

Sandy was not my friend. She had no friends, he saw to that. Poor tiny, timid mouse. But she was a person, kind and good where she could be. She was not always a tired wife, scurrying back from the shop with the mean buying his boozing would allow.

Her life has gone. Just like that. On a whim, an action, not even a thought. He didn't even plan it. Just an impulse. She is ended, gone in the time it takes for him to grab her head and push her down. And hold her there until her nose and throat, lungs and soul fill up with bitter beer. Just an impulse. Not even a thought.

What joy to be a wife. Once she must have loved him. It would be too bitter if she never did.

Should we be bringing these thin souls to justice? To court? To a jury of their peers? What joke is this?

Action is required. I must chart a course. I will help Ted. I will help Sandy. He has decided me, this hand that held her under.

Coburn is conspiring. I can feel it. He has that look about him, slightly apprehensive and slightly triumphant. How can he find the time? He should be too busy.

"What's been your progress on Sean Porter?"

"Oh, he's around, boss. I don't have an address for him yet but he's active on the Strip. He's got a boyfriend. A real estate developer. Got a bit of money apparently. Well, flashes it about anyway."

"Get an address. Don't call me boss. Sam, what have you got?"

"Nothing from the local marina people. They've never heard of any relatives or of Sean Porter. One thing they did say though. On the day that Ryan Porter went missing the guy who runs the slip there saw two men trying to put one of those big ski boats in the water. He thought it was funny because they didn't know what they were doing and it fell off the trailer. Described them as one Caucasian male in his late thirties, dark hair, average height. Was wearing a panama hat and white jeans. Who would wear a panama hat in a ski boat? The second man, also Caucasian, late twenties, brown hair, very good looking. Looked like a male model, according to the slip man, who thought they were both probably gay, well, poofters he said.

"He did remember the boat a bit better. Said it was a ski boat, about seven metres long, metal flake-blue with lime-green flames painted along the stern. Inboard engine, looked and sounded like a V8. No registration number that he could remember but it was called *Phantasy* with a ph.

"I didn't talk to him earlier because he was away on holidays. Only came back this week. No one at Farley's Marine had heard of Sean Porter or knew anything about two men in a blue ski boat."

Cameron is thoughtful.

"Not the sort of boat you would use if you were trying to be discreet."

Nguyen says, "Yeah, but remember we don't know if they were planning to kill the old guy or if it just happened. Anyway, we don't even know it was Sean and his boyfriend. What is he? A real estate developer? Sounds like a wanker's boat. Lime-green flames. What sort of boats do developers have, sergeant?"

Cameron is non-committal.

"Jamie, what have you found at the Securities Commission? Any leads on Porter's money?"

"Oh, yes, ma'am. I've found his lawyer."

He grins at Nguyen.

"The only place I could find Porter's name was as director of a company called AB Red Pty Ltd, whose registered address was at 25 Lindgard St in the city. At 25 Lindgard St are the rooms of one M. J. Castigleone, solicitor. Very small, very neat, very private. One secretary and that's it. Mr Castigleone was unwilling to discuss any of Mr Porter's business except to say that he had extensive holdings. He would not disclose what they were. AB Red was only one of a number of companies. He also said that he was not Porter's only solicitor and he believed that the work had been spread around.

"One interesting thing. He knew Ryan was dead and said that everything he owned was owned jointly with Ted Jones. So now it's all Ted's, who came to see him about ten days ago. Wouldn't say why Ted came or what he wanted and was quite firm about getting me out of the office."

Coburn is feeling excluded by all this.

"What does this company, AB Red, do?"

"Manufacturing. At least that's what's listed with the Commission. According to Castigleone it makes some kind of plastic pipes. Apparently Ryan came up with the engineering specs and now they use these pipes instead of timber for wharves and pontoons. The company looks quite successful. Its before-tax profit last year was just under a million. The factory itself is on the Gold Coast. Lots of wharves up there, I guess. I called and spoke to the general manager who had never heard of Ryan Porter or Ted Jones. All his dealings had been with Castigleone."

There is a moment's silence as we all let this sink in. Cameron breaks it.

"It's weird. Those two old guys are loaded. If there are lots of other companies like AB Red making million dollar profits every year, then they are seriously loaded. Yet they don't seem to give a damn about it. I mean, it may explain the *Annie Marie* and the money spent on her but it doesn't explain why they lived in that hovel eating kangaroo."

I wrap it up.

"But it does explain why Sean and partner may have been interested in visiting Uncle Ryan. If indeed they did. Coburn, stop messing about and find Sean Porter. Sam, you help him and remember, keep it quiet until we know some more about him and the boyfriend. Jamie, get up to the Gold Coast and check out AB Red. It probably won't give us anything but we are a little short of leads. Cameron, get onto the

Maritime Services Board and see if they have any records for a metal flake-blue boat with lime-green flames."

Coburn is shifty. Something is going on. Is it this case or has he entered into another conspiracy with some like-minded piece of corruption?

"What's going to happen with Valentine? Seems to me there hasn't been much work done there. After all, she knew where the body was. A little more pressure in that area could work."

His colouring betrays him. The flush rises up his neck. What does he know, or think he knows?

"If you have a problem with how the case is running then I suggest you make a written complaint, sergeant. If not, get off your tush and do some work."

But he hasn't finished yet. He tosses this in as an aside while Orr and Nguyen are leaving the room.

"By the way, I heard from Hornsby. Masterson's out. Bailed. Guess drowning your wife is no big deal these days, huh."

Although it's for the wrong reasons, Coburn is right. I have to push harder on Valentine. I have been resisting. I do not want to see her. And I do. I want to see her more than anything. I am both terrified and attracted. I hide in the only refuge I have, my job. I must see her because she is a suspect at worst, a witness at best.

A flock of pelicans wheels above me as my little boat putt putts across to her island. The birds are huge, their wingspans must be nearly two metres. They are riding the thermals and circle higher and higher without moving a wing. They tuck their long necks back into their shoulders. They look so easy, so relaxed up there. Only the crik in my neck finally stops me watching them.

There is no sign of her as I climb over the ridge towards the house. As I walk past a small clump of trees a pig squeals and comes rushing out towards me. I stop dead. I don't know much about pigs and it is big.

It stops by my left knee, raises its flat snout up to sniff, then snorts. This exchange wakes up the dogs who were asleep on the sandstone verandah of the house. They come galloping across the valley towards me. The pig is somewhat put off by this sudden onslaught and trots back into the trees, ears flapping.

The dogs are friendly and inquisitive. I am thoroughly sniffed and rubbed. By the time I reach the house Valentine has emerged. She must have been asleep. Her hair is tousled and she has the soft, vulnerable look of the newly awakened.

"I wondered when you were coming back. Cup of tea?"

We go inside. I don't know if it's because she was sleeping but she is relaxed and affable.

"How's the investigation going? Any lucky breaks or hidden clues?"

"Why did you go looking for Porter's body? Was it just because Cameron asked you? Why did you spend all that time out there looking for him?"

"I've been through all this."

"Go through it again."

She pushes a mug towards me across the table and sits down. Sighs. "I don't know really. I kept having dreams, well, nightmares, about his body falling through the water. I became a bit obsessed. As though I had no choice. I just had to keep going until I found him."

"Don't you find that a little unusual, odd even? That someone would do that? Become obsessed about finding a body. After all, he was only your friend, he wasn't, I don't know, anything closer, was he?"

She goes still, flat.

"This is the river. Odd things are normal here."

"Why did it take you so long to find him?"

"The currents are like that. You can drop an orange in the water and three days later it can be five miles up stream. Or bobbing out on the ocean. I've been here most of my adult life and I can't tell what the river is going to do. I was lucky it didn't take longer."

"So you have no idea of where he went in?"

"No."

I walk over to the sink bench and stare out the window. I can see the slope behind the house running up to a grove of red twisted trees at the top.

"Jones and Porter are something of a mystery to us. I can understand their desire to be alone, cut off from everything but … The *Annie Marie* is spotless. You couldn't find a boat that was better taken care of yet their home is a hovel. Apart from the launch they appear to be very poor but we find that they are extremely wealthy. They have paid no personal income tax, claimed no pensions, only Porter had a driver's licence. Their affairs appear to be managed by a number of solicitors who do not know each other. This is highly secretive behaviour. Why? Why were these two men like this?"

"I don't know. I didn't know they had money until after Ryan died. The *Annie Marie* ... They've always had a big boat that they have taken care of. I think it was their security, their escape route if anything ever went bad again. Some people are like that. It doesn't mean anything. That's just the way they are."

"I'm not trying to judge them. I'm trying to understand why one of them is dead with his head smashed in."

I'm explaining myself to her. This is turning into a conversation.

"Have you ever seen a big ski boat, metal flake-blue with lime-green flames on the stern. Called *Phantasy*, with a ph?"

"No. But it shouldn't be hard to miss. If I do see it I'll let you know. Why? Whose is it?"

I make another attempt to take back the initiative.

"Most people are killed by someone in their family and it's usually over money."

"It isn't my area of expertise."

She just sits there and stares back at me. On the wall behind her there is a colour photograph, unframed, roughly tacked up. It looks uncared for, an odd note in this polished home. It is of a woman who looks to be in her sixties, face aglow with rosacea. She is wearing a faded floral print dress, walking in front of an old, unpainted woolshed, stock yards stretching away to one side. In each hand is an iced pound cake. The camera has caught her unprepared and she has looked up just as the shutter clicked. Her face is tired, worn down with a particular rural stoicism compounded with poor education and low intelligence.

Valentine turns to see what I am looking at. When she turns back I gesture toward the picture.

"Who is that?"

"I don't know specifically. In general, she's everything I have run away from. Everything I loathe. Contrary to urban belief there is no romance in agriculture, only dullness, resentment and a vicious nationalism. She is my reminder."

"But you live here. This is country."

"This is an island in a river. And it's mine."

The currents of anger and bitterness swirl out of her. Whatever she has left behind to come here is still boiling inside. I am nervous. She is too powerful, too strong and implacable. Any path I may climb with this woman will be steep indeed. And will the view from the top be worth the struggle?

I walk outside and stand on the verandah looking out across the gardens. I feel her come and stand behind me. She is very close. I can smell her, soft and warm like flannelette sheets. I don't want this job. I want to go up the old men's creek and become a hermit.

She puts her hand on my shoulder and her breath tickles my ear.

"If you are looking for justice, it will be done. If you are looking to write a report and close a file you will be waiting a long time."

I turn towards her. She is inches from me, wearing (what else?) a singlet and shorts. All I can see are those blue eyes, so sharp and clean. My pulse is hammering, thundering in my temples but I can't move. All those years of control, those habits of denial are far too strong to break yet, just for a river girl with blue eyes. I am frozen, I couldn't move if I wanted to.

There is a shift in her eyes. Fear or disapointment. I can't tell. Her hand drops away and she steps back. Her walls are just as high as mine.

And then we stand there, a pair of fools. The tension so strong in the air I wonder that it isn't coloured. I wait to leave as though something else is going to pick me up and carry me back down the hill. She doesn't help. Just ducks her head like some shy schoolgirl and traces the shape of a paving stone with her bare toe.

I have to leave but I can't. I want to stay but I can't. How does anybody ever do this? The absurdity finally shakes me loose and I turn away towards the path. It is all I can do not to stumble. A couple of dogs jump up and rush past me. I can't look back, I can't afford to. I concentrate what remaining discipline I have on getting back to the wharf without stumbling, falling, or crawling in the dirt in front of her.

I pray that Cameron's little boat will start and it does. When I get back to my car I am trembling so badly I can barely get the keys into the ignition.

I don't go back to the office. I stop at the bottle shop by the drycleaners and buy two bottles of Cardhu and a bag of ice.

Back in my flat I settle down on the floor in the corner opposite the balcony, glass, ice and liquor before me. The carpet is thin and gray and before long not even the scotch can stop me feeling the concrete. I begin to imagine that I am sitting on the bones of the building, everything stripped bare and exposed.

The thing I fear most about love is the vulnerability. No matter how many times I may tell myself that degradation need not automatically follow surrender, the terror that it might is enough.

Like the steel girders and concrete slabs of an empty high-rise, will the skeleton of my self be left naked and showing for all the world to see as the sun burns and the rain freezes the emptiness of my life?

Despite my appreciation of single malts, I seldom drink. I haven't counted the glasses but the level in the first bottle doesn't seem to have dropped that much and already the shape of the room has changed. It has stretched and altered like the safe parameters of my life. Sentimentality is sneaking into my veins with the alcohol.

It occurs to me that walking away from her like that was rude. A breach of good manners if nothing else and I am ashamed. Guilty. Mortifed that I may have caused her pain through my obsession for self-protection.

Why did I bother to buy two bottles when a few inches from one can dissolve me into self-pitying maudlin nonsense? Even my capacity for alcoholic self-abasement is strictly limited.

Only halfway through the bottle and I have to crawl to the bathroom to vomit.

I have been sitting here for some time. The bathroom tiles are regular and orderly, pleasing. They shine in the light. The grouting is clean and white. I have never been able to tolerate grubby bathrooms.

An apology is required. I should never have just walked away from her without so much as a single word.

The shower clears my head suprisingly quickly. In the steam and the heat, the alcohol evaporates like so much useless vapour.

I dress carefully. I am going to apologise.

A soft drizzle wets the road and the world is dark. The asphalt flows before me, a black glistening river taking me out of the city. There is little traffic, soft shining shapes slipping in and out of the edges of the cars' lights. The lack of traffic is a brief puzzle until I pass a random breath-testing crew packing up. I have no idea what the time is. I must have been sitting on the bathroom floor for hours. A little earlier and I might have been charged with drink-driving.

The trip down to the river is slow. My driving is cautious, the RBT crew at the back of my mind. The city recedes and the freeway drops down through the escarpment. In the darkness a train, carriages lit up, flickers through the bush, running parallel to the road. It is pounding down to the river, like me. Lost in the night, like me.

The blue light flashes in my rearview mirror before I hear the siren. Rushing and urgent the patrol car is wailing in the lane next to me. My foot drops away from the pedal and my stomach cramps. But it doesn't want me. It speeds past, on down the hill, blue noise bouncing back off the sandstone cuttings.

A breakdown bay comes up in the headlights and I pull over. I get the door open just in time. Vomit splatters on the wet tarmac. When the shaking and cramping finally stop I get the car started again. I am going to apologise.

The river finally appears, a deeper, darker blackness. I turn off before the bridge and take the road between the railway tracks and the water. The rain has stopped but the street lights here are only occasional. The pub and the railway station are both empty, desolate in the wet light.

At the marina the car park is deserted and the gate to the pontoons is locked. Cameron's little boat rocks gently on the other side of a chain link fence topped with barbed wire. The police boat is tied up behind its own wharf, equally impenetrable. The dark shadows are quiet and still, empty of boats and people. Only the channel markers wink erratically in the distance.

Walking east, the sea wall ends and I slip on the wet rocks. There are oyster shells and mud. This is her river. This quiet deep blackness that stretches out in front of me is hers. I can see the distant shape of her island, a different quality in the darkness. The clouds are clearing and the lights of an airliner wink as it heads south to the city I have just left.

Sitting on the flattest rock at the river's edge I take my shoes off and put my feet in the water. It's warm, so tepid I can hardly feel it.

Fear has always slipped around my life, defining and moulding the borders of my actions. It has pushed me forward and held me back. As a child I believed that adulthood meant the absence of fear but I found instead, as I progressed towards this once desirable state, that fear simply became more shaded and subtle. And increasingly powerful. Sometimes it seems that everything I have ever done has been about facing or surrendering to it. I prefer to face it. Then, at least, I can hold at bay that other seduction, the temptation to wallow in self-contempt.

There have been people I have known, both men and women, who have, on rare occasions, called me brave. I have never really understood what they meant. I have only ever prevailed against my terrors through a lack of choice. There has been no other alternative, nothing else to do. For me this is not courage, it is inevitability. Perhaps it is as simple as having a personal definition of right and wrong. If something is right then it must be done. Once the die is cast there is little to be gained by prevarication. Is this courage?

By the time I have my pants and shirt off and I am in the water, I almost have my fear of drowning under control. I can swim. A good middle class upbringing saw to that.

I enter her river because I must be in her life. I have no idea how far it is. I have no idea if I'm going to make it or drown. If I can do this, this one terrifying thing, then my life will mean something other than a well ordered file.

I have never taken a real risk, the kind that has offered me a choice—the chance to refuse and back away. She is worth having and I will trust her black river like I must trust her. Or spend the rest of my life never able to drink more than half a bottle of scotch.

So I float and wonder. Will this warm salty water become as much a part of my life as it is hers? It is benign at the moment. I could be floating in amniotic fluid. Death comes in a warm bath. I gently paddle toward the hump in the distance and concentrate on relaxing my jaw. I am going to apologise.

The swimming is not difficult. The river seems to be carrying me in the right direction. Something brushes against my leg and my heart stops. I spin around in the water. I can see nothing. The surface of the water ripples around me, too dark to see into.

What am I doing? The absurdity of it all finally hits and I start to laugh but water keeps getting in my mouth and I have to stop. I have come quite a way. It is as far forward as it is back. Who cares if I can only handle half a bottle of scotch? I tasted every drop.

If this is the only risk I am ever going to take then I am damn well going to make sure I survive it.

I strike out with a little more vigour, pushing myself to make strong even strokes. There is a beach on the south side of the island and I can soon see the cliffs above it. Then the current changes and I feel some kind of eddy pushing me sideways across the island. Anxiety creeps through my gut. I stop and force myself to relax, treading water, slow breaths. I cannot afford to cramp up out here. It will kill me.

When I have the panic under control I realise that the water, while carrying me across the beach is also taking me towards it. I strike out again and my hand hits something soft. Before I can stop I am surrounded by soft lumps of something. One catches on my fingers and I lift my hand out of the water. They are jelly fish. Harmless, I hope.

The next thing I hit is the bottom. Mud, soft, warm and welcome. I can stand. In fact the water is only waist deep. As I stumble and wade onto the harder sand I wonder just how deep it was. Could I have been desperately swimming for my life in water no more than three feet deep?

The air is colder than the water. I have no clothes and no idea how to get from this tiny beach to her house.

Valentine

It was the dogs that found her. I was working in the bakery when I heard them barking from the back bay. They once trapped a drowning wallaby there and I assumed it had happened again, so torch and knife in hand I ran up to the cliffs and down the path that I have never finished making.

And here she is. In the torchlight she is shivering and looking as dignified and beautiful as anyone standing, in bra and knickers, wet on a beach in the early hours of the morning possibly could.

I am astounded, aghast. Lost for words, which is okay as she seems to have something to say.

"I have come to apologise for my rudeness earlier today. I should never have left like that and I am sorry if I caused you …"

"Yesterday."

"Sorry?"

"It was yesterday."

"Oh. I don't have my watch. I was unsure of the time. I realise this is somewhat unusual but the gate to the marina was locked and I wanted to talk to you."

She was unsure of the time. Well, fancy that. Here she is, all wet and wasted from her feat and she is unsure of the time. Bugger me. A wonderful girl like this, pernickety and neat, should have a timepiece for all occasions. I forebear to comment.

"I am very glad you've come however you got here. Would you like to come up to the house and get warm?"

"Thank you."

She walks past me, gleaming white in the night, and follows the dogs onto the path. Fancy that. Just fancy that!

I have never in all my life wanted so much to laugh, to throw myself to the ground and roll around hooting. For joy, for wonder, for sheer bloody amazement. To jump and fly, to somersault through the air. To leap and holler in delight. But I don't think it would be well received at the moment.

She swam here. She got in the water in the middle of the night and swam here. I give silent and sincere thanks to my wonderful river for an outgoing tide and eastward current across the south shoals. If I give the river what is hers she will give me back that which is mine.

By the time we get home she is shaking badly and turning blue. I put her in a hot bath and heat up yesterday's left-over soup. I think she has been drinking. She has the oddly concentrated but unfocused air of someone who is unusually drunk. Not that I care. She can get as plastered as she wants if it means she is going to come to me with her defences down. Swimming!

Warm now, wrapped up in an old jumper and some trackie pants, she sits at the table drinking soup. I keep grinning at her. I just can't help myself. Putting her spoon down she fixes me with those grey eyes, defensive and just a tad embarrassed.

"Don't laugh at me."

"I'm not laughing at you. I'm happy. I've never been so happy. I think you're amazing, incredible, wonderful. I can't believe you did that."

Slowly, slowly, her face relaxes. Shoulders drop and the tension eases away. All that control and discipline, the carefully held facade of dignity, collapses. Elbows on the table, she drops her face in her hands and moans.

"Oh, god. I got drunk. I felt so bad about you, so tense and all churned up. I haven't been drunk in years, since I was a kid. You're a witness in a case and I can't stop thinking about you.This has never happened to me before and I don't know what to do. I hate the water. It terrifies me. I've always believed I will drown. I kept throwing up on the road."

Head up now she stretches her hands across the table. We're holding hands and grinning at each other like a couple of sideshow clowns waiting for ping pong balls.

"What are we going to do?"

She's asking me? Like I would know.

"Well, right now, I've got baking to do. I have to make deliveries this morning. You should probably go to bed and sleep it off. Or you can come down to the bakery with me."

My lovely grey-eyed, quietly reserved cop sits, arms around her knees, on bags of durum wheat, and talks. And talks and talks. When she lets go this girl doesn't mess about. She tells me about her childhood as I knead the fruit doughs, her parents while I stoke the oven, the police academy as I weigh out the rolls. By the time everything is baked and stacked in the baskets on the flying fox, she has been through the loneliness and isolation of her job. And is nearly asleep.

I start the winch on the flying fox and send the bread down to the wharf. I help her up off the bags of flour and walk her to the house. The sun is just coming up over the cliffs that separate the river from the sea.

She slips into bed with barely a murmur, on her side, knees up, hands tucked up by her chin. I touch her cheek and she holds my hand, turns it and kisses the palm. Then she looks up at me and smiles with such simple trust that I almost stop breathing.

"Come back soon."

"I will. I promise."

This morning my tinnie flies, barely touching the river. This morning the river runs the tides with me, speeding me on my way. This morning the world is mine. This morning is perfect.

When I get home the miracle is real. She is still there. She wakes up so easily. I kiss her on the mouth, soft. Her arms steal around my waist and my hands alight on her shoulders. Her bare skin is warm, almost hot. We kiss again, for longer. Then stop. And stare. Just to look. Just to see the other and delight in it.

Her body engrosses me. She is smooth and pale in sharp contrast to my tanned and stringy muscles. When I slide in beside her, we fit.

We are unified in intense and exclusive concentration. Her body is my landscape and I am hers. There is no rushing, no trickery. We both take all the time we want. We have nowhere else to go, nothing but this to do. For us the clocks have slowed.

My lovely cop has given me her body, her lovely white dreamboat of a body. All breasts and wetness, all thighs and cunt. What a girl. What a lover.

I am a happy hermit.

I am in love.

I can smell her skin on mine. I can feel her swollen lips on my fingers. I have traced her scarlet cunt with my tongue. I have dwelt inside her. I have worshipped at the temple of desire and been repaid a thousandfold. She brought herself to me and I have cupped her, warm, with my hands.

My swimmer.

And if I plunge, sliding down the slope of her breast, if I smooth the puckers of her skin, of her soft pink nipple, if I slip my hands beneath her rump and pull her tight against me, will she stay? If the palm of my hand rubs wet and foaming between her thighs will she swim back for good?

Will she? Should she? What if she does? Do I plan to share? Will I spread my hands wide and offer her all this, my home, my island, my fortress?

This is all it takes. A swimmer. Grey eyes and a quiet smile and I roll, tummy up. Docile and doglike. I love you. You are my person. I will devote my life to you. This is me? I can do this?

Oh, wretched creature. All those years of defences, of isolation, of carefully sustained withdrawal, gone. Tumbled. Crashed in a moment for a woman from a profession I despise. Corrupters, beaters, the mindless violence of petty authority. The warfare past of mine and theirs. The queers, the perverts, the dykes and the drags. Us against them. And they always wore blue. This is where she swam from, my lovely girl.

Even if I do humble myself, expose my dreams and longings and spread wide my generous arms, if I offer her my life and all my worldly goods, will she take us? Does she want a dozen dogs? Or will she turn her head away to hide the start, the surprise, the shock? She will say, kindly, that I have misunderstood her intentions. She had no thought of a relationship, of a staying togetherness. She simply found me interesting, eccentric perhaps, but nothing more.

Why am I doing this? This is madness. It would be better to brace the boat and return to the madness on the water then to continue this kind of lunacy. Enough. I am accustomed to great tasks. I have work to do.

There are two commitments you have made, Valentine. And neither are to her. One to Sandy, one to Ted. They must be done. They must be planned, crafted and carried out.

And what will she do when she finds out? When she knows that you have given her your body but not your intentions. When she knows that you have been less than honest, less than open about your plans for the future.

A true love. How can I lie to a true love? And even if I am not hers then surely she is mine. So the lie is no less, whether it belongs only to me or to us.

Stewart

Usually I dislike Friday evenings. I find most recreation boring and irrelevant. The weekend stretches long and useless before me. Empty time to be filled. Saturday and Sunday are long flat vistas of waiting. Waiting for Monday, or maybe, if I'm lucky, a call to a weekend case. Friday evening — when more rounded mortals adjourn to the pub, to their families, to whatever kind of oblivion they choose. But not for me. I wait for Monday.

Or used to. Tomorrow morning I am going back to the river and her island. By boat. The river girl is waiting for me. How can so many things have changed so much so quickly? When I remember that night I am still a little startled at myself. More often than should happen, I catch myself staring into space with a child's smirk on my face.

So this Friday evening I sort my files and clear my desk slowly. Orr's report on his useless Gold Coast trip the last to go away. This sense of anticipation, half fear, half delight, is something I wish to savour.

A movement on the other side of the darkened glass distracts me. Nguyen. He comes in, but seems reluctant.

"Sorry, ma'am. I didn't realise you were leaving."

Yes he did. I leave at this time every Friday. Nguyen is troubled.

"What's the problem, Sam?"

He clears his throat and shuffles a bit. We are both standing.

"Just why did you send me off with Coburn, ma'am? I mean, was there anything specific you wanted?"

"I want you to find Sean Porter."

"Well, that's it, ma'am. We don't seem to be."

"What do you mean?"

"I've been hanging around the Strip with Coburn for three days now but we don't actually do anything. I mean ... it's weird. I know he's a sergeant and everything but we don't seem to do any work. We've just been driving around, drinking in a few clubs, straight ones, and chatting with a few of Coburn's snitches. But he's not asking them anything. Which is okay, I guess, but there's something else."

"Mmm?"

"See, there's this woman I know, she's a dyke and she works in one of the gay clubs on the Strip. Well, she's my cousin, actually. Anyway, I went to see her. She says Coburn came in there about two weeks ago with Porter. She knows Porter 'cause he did a bit of barwork for them but got the flick. He was pulling trade when he was supposed to be pouring. She gave me his address.

"See, that's it, ma'am. Coburn knows Porter. She said they seemed to know each other well and Porter was nervous, scared even. But Coburn hasn't let on. Has he? I mean, if he's told you but you're holding it for some reason then that would be different. Wouldn't it?"

I sink back into my chair. Nguyen becomes increasingly uncomfortable. Outside the main office is almost deserted. Cameron and Orr are still there. Orr is looking towards us. He obviously knows why Nguyen is here.

"Get those two in here."

"Yes, ma'am."

Cameron comes in with a printout in her hand. Sam tells her what he told me. I was right. Orr already knows.

The four of us sit and wait for it to filter through all the layers of suspicion in any cop's mind.

Cameron begins.

"A shakedown, maybe. Coburn puts the hard word on Sean for a payoff. Hand over x amount and I'll forget I ever found you."

Orr plays devil's advocate.

"Just 'cos the guy's a living fossil doesn't mean he's corrupt. Maybe he's just holding onto the info to get some kind of advantage. Those old-style cops do that stuff. You know, knowledge is power. I know where the suspect is so I have more power than you do."

"Power to do what, though? At our last meeting the boss asked what his progress was. He said he didn't have the address. That was a lie. He must have had it."

Sam is feeling guilty.

"I feel really bad about this but for the last three days I've been sitting on my butt wasting time with this guy. He goes through half a bottle of scotch before lunch, for Chrissake. Not that it shows."

Cameron has a specific inquiry.

"What is the address?"

"Twenty-four Fitzroy Crescent, Surry Hills."

"Boss, look at this. I just got this out of the MSB computer half an hour ago. It has taken me nearly all week to find it. Boats aren't listed by their name or colour, it's by length and engine size. *Phantasy*, 8 metre, V8 ski boat, metal flake-blue, is registered to a company called Danelli Holdings, address, 24 Fitzroy Crescent, Surry Hills."

"My cousin said that Porter's boyfriend was a Steve Danelli. She didn't know what he did but apparently he's kind of flash. You know, mobile phone, BMW, etc."

Three eager faces hot on the scent. Coburn, like most corrupt cops, is lazy and incompetent. He would rather beat a confession out of a suspect than search a room to find the evidence. But he has been on the force a long time and is not without allies. After all, he made sergeant. Someone is looking after him.

"Okay. First thing Monday — Jamie, do a search on Danelli Holdings, in particular their finances. I want to know if Mr Danelli has money troubles. Sam, leave Coburn alone. He's not going to make any moves with you tagging along.

"Alice, pull Coburn's file from personnel, discreetly. See who his snitches are, whether he's ever pulled any loan sharks or bad money people. We'll have the next case conference on Wednesday. Before then I want every little thing any of you have found out in the interim. As far as Coburn's concerned this meeting has never taken place. And don't call me boss. Have a good weekend."

And I do. I put aside my depressing concerns about Coburn and have a weekend of quiet desire and fulfilment. And laughter. She makes me laugh.

There is a kind of bliss in the domesticity of the beloved. In the easiness of it all. In the warmth of her house the coldness of my apartment disappears.

In the night if we roll apart we reach out to draw the other back. Curled around her back, my face against her shoulder blade, I breathe in the scent of her skin. Her body is a puzzle, profoundly familiar while infinitely astonishing. I am assiduous in my exploration.

Here, in the middle of the river that is beginning to seduce me too, I feel human. Larger, kinder, perhaps, than just my job. She is so rich and abundant. My years of self-discipline and control stretch behind me in thin contrast.

My life has been a narrow search for the provable. That which can only be interpreted one way. I have not sought to decide guilt or innocence. Only what I can prove. I have tested the quality of everything I have ever known. And I am good at it. The sunshine and the garden and the dogs and her gleaming golden skin do not make me question my abilities. They make me question the culture I use them in.

She takes me across to the north side of the river and on a path up over the escarpment. We follow wallaby trails through the bush. Behind is the river laid out in all its curves and Byzantine twists. Its mystery is seductive, a story rewritten daily, a muddy palimpsest always renewed and always the same. Before us is the ocean.

She leads me down a path which follows the face of a cliff. We scramble under sandstone overhangs and across huge boulders. At the bottom is a tiny bay. White sand without a footprint on it. A reef further out catches the surf. Here the water is still and clear. I can see the sand on the bottom. I am not afraid of water like this. She refuses to believe that I am afraid of water but she holds my hand as we wade in.

My love and I go swimming in the cold green sea.

Valentine

Joy is a real thing. I go rambling on the river in the dark. A full moon, the siren's song, bold and yellow, calls me forth. The kayak is best for this, the seduction of its slim shape whispering through the water. And somehow the river seems to hold itself so still on these occasions. The surface smooth and clear, dark and shining with the moon reflected like a drowning dream.

I can feel it then, a current through my body. I wonder if I could feel this now, so real, so solid if my childhood had been easier. If my safety, security, here on this great rollicking river is as true and tempered as it is because I never dreamt it was attainable.

I know, of course, that I will fight to keep this. A religious who cannot cease to believe. My faith is the water and the flow of the tides. This salt green stuff that carries a million beings in every great drop. Who needs a god when you can believe in the glowing dark of the water? When I sit here, still and floating, my craft a speck on the face of the river, I am as ancient and primitive as the cliffs, as immutable as the river bed.

I will fight to keep this. A fierce and violent song swells in me and I feed it on these nights when the face of the moon flattens the water with yellow light. Mine is a wild and rampaging heart.

Mine is not the only blood in song with the sky. The dogs are howling, their voices ringing from the angophoras at the top of the bluff. We are a chorus of guardians, a warrior breed, our trumpets our own.

Stewart

On Monday I enter Danelli's name in the computer. He was once picked up on suspicion of dealing but wasn't charged. It was seven years ago in Darlinghurst. The officer who interrogated him was Senior Constable Michael Chambers.

I call Fargo in to my office.

"Tom, have you ever come across a Steve Danelli? Darlinghurst, drugs, maybe?"

He swings back in the swivel chair, hand rubbing his chin.

"Nope, don't think so. Why?"

"What about a Michael Chambers? He was a Senior seven years ago."

"Mick Chambers. Sure, I knew him. He was an old mate of Coburn's. The two Micks they used to call them. They were both back in Darlo together. They had the same initials. Used to work together."

I put my elbows up on the desk and lean towards him.

"What were their reputations?"

"As in clean or dirty? Well, Chambers was a bit smelly. Used to spend a bit more time up at the Cross than he really had to. Coburn was in his shadow a bit. The follower rather than the leader. Chambers used to talk big about his snitches but nothing much ever came of it. You know, whispers about jobs or deals that we would get close to then they'd just disappear. I always thought Chambers was leading a bit of dance, myself, but there was never anything you could really put your finger on."

"Where is Chambers now?"

"Dead. Died in a diving accident in the Solomon Islands about four years ago. I always thought it was a bit fishy."

He smirks at his joke and leans back in the chair. He runs his hands through his hair. The woman on his left forearm gyrates with the movement of his muscles.

"What are you looking for, ma'am? If you don't mind my asking?"

Fargo is shrewd and tough but this isn't his case.

"Nothing in particular, Tom. I'm just trying to get some background straight. Ask Alice Cameron to come in will you? And ask her to bring the file I told her to pull on Friday."

He gives a quick grin, cheeky and confident. The door sighs shut behind him. Seven years ago the Patrol Commander at Darlinghurst was Inspector Ray Matthews. A smart cop on the rise. Who may well be much closer to Mick Coburn than he wanted me to believe. I wonder if he knows Danelli. And if I ask him will he tell me?

Cameron looks harried as she slips into the chair Fargo has just vacated.

"I haven't had much time to look at this yet, ma'am. I've been helping Orr with the search on Danelli Holdings."

"And what have you found?"

"Not much really. The registered office is the same address in Fitzroy Crescent but they don't seem to have filed any returns for the last four years. The company directors are listed as Steve Danelli and a Michael Chambers."

I can feel the key to the puzzle gleaming just beyond the reach of my outstretched hand. In that brief tiny moment I forget to breathe and the pain snake slides through my gut.

It's not possible. How stupid can they be? A cop and a suspected drug dealer owning a company together. And what does it have to do with Ryan Porter?

"What does this company, Danelli Holdings, do?"

"Real estate from the look of it, ma'am. Although they don't seem to be very good at it. The last posted profit from four years back was only three hundred and eighty dollars before tax. The assets they listed are a couple of apartment buildings in Redfern and the place in Fitzroy Crescent. Maybe it's just a tax dodge."

"Find out if the company still owns those two apartment blocks. See if you can find who they bank with. If there's a letting agent for the flats they will have an account to pay into. Try and dig out Danelli's current financial status. If Danelli needs money and Sean told him about Uncle Ryan we may have some answers. Don't spend any time on Chambers. I know where he is. And you can leave Coburn's file here."

"Yes, ma'am."

"Send Fargo back in, will you. Oh, and make arrangements to return the *Annie Marie* to Jones. The Water Police want their dock back and we don't really need it any longer. "

When Fargo returns he has the look. Something is happening and he wants in. It's written in neon all over his face.

"I need some watching done. Unofficial. No local faces. It's a case you're not on."

"Sure. How many targets?"

"Two."

Fargo has an extensive acquaintance. For this job we are going to need outsiders.

"Round the clock will be tough. Is there a budget?"

"Of course not. This is not happening. There's a house in Fitzroy Crescent, Surry Hills. I want a record of who's in and who's out. No contact, just observation and it better be good. The other's a bit more delicate. I want a tail on Mick Coburn."

The energy in his face fades. He is not so eager for this part.

"Isn't that a job for IAD? Something official."

"Do you trust IAD, Tom?"

He shifts in the seat, ducks his head across his shoulder.

"Well, no, but ... "

"I'm not doing this on a whim. And there are reasons I can't go further up the line. You're a smart boy and I need you."

I've never asked him for something quite like this before. All the cop's loyalties, both misguided and justified, jostle within him. I wait. And wait. And then he comes to me of his own free will.

"Okay. What do you need?"

"Three watchers. When he goes home to sleep so can they. When he's here you can keep a quiet eye on him. I want a rundown on everyone he meets and where he goes. If he turns up at the Fitzroy Crescent house I want to know immediately. No watchers in the office. You can include their reports with your usual stuff so nothing looks out of the ordinary. And no one, but no one, knows about this."

"Yes, ma'am."

He rises and leaves my office a little slower than he came in. I am now as vulnerable to him as he is to me.

Valentine

There are great and mighty tasks before me. In the midst of my usual folding of dough and feeding of yeasts I have some killing to do. Killing I believe to be fair and just. Housekeeping, cleaning up. The fulfilment of promises.

I am nervous, apprehensive. A little anxious about the future. I am no fool, no stupid unthinking innocent. I know that my lovely cop will find out. And she will be torn in two.

After I have done this I will be different.

In the darkness my kayak disappears. Its pale golden fibreglass takes on the blackness of the night. As we slip across the dark river, my little boat and I, we reflect the sky. The black sky, the sky with moon and stars, and the dark velvet sky without. I can slip by you as quiet as a whisper, not even a shadow, not even that extra deepness of the dark, to show that I am there.

Invisible and silent I paddle up past the northern face of Top Island. There are no houses here, no roads. This is just the river, pure and primitive. This is my place. There are no boats, no night traffic, no winking greens and reds. The night is mine and I will use it. Around the western tip of the island and into the inlet.

Here the road passes just behind the mangroves and the lights of the houses glow behind the trees. There are not many. This is not prime real estate. Only those whose choices have been closed down could love this spot. Perched between the road and the railway line. The roar of trains behind and the mangroves and mud before. A place for those without choices — for Sandy.

The boat slides across the mud to rest between the mangrove roots. I leave it nestled there with the paddle and slip across the road. There are none to see and none that could.

Up the concrete drive by the side of the house and around the back. The kitchen door is open. It is a warm and mild night. I stand outside the pool of light and watch him. He is sitting at the kitchen table with his back to the door. There are bottles and plates piled on every surface. And a nasty, rotten smell.

I step into the doorway. I can see him reflected in the glass of the hall door in front of me. He does not know I am there. He is busy. There are magazines strewn across the filthy plates and on the floor. One-handed reading. All women. Women tied up, women tied down. Women untied. He is wearing a pair of dirty underpants. In his left hand is a woman spread-eagled on a rug the same colour as her pubic hair. In his right hand is his penis.

With his hair I pull his head back smoothly, firmly, and cut his throat. He is dead in seconds, blood pouring across his belly. His right hand convulses and tightens on his penis. His head tips back, empty eyes gazing at the ceiling.

I have touched nothing but him. Stepped only on the thin blue rug that protects the lino. There is no blood, no mark on me. I leave. There is nothing to show I was there.

I rinse my knife in the river. In the dark cleansing water of my river. My little boat and I slip away through the darkness. I have to set my yeasts for tomorrow's baking.

The rain is streaming on the windows as we pause in the mud to look at this big black thing. The weather has turned as it is wont to do at this time of the year. There has been water in the air for the past three days. Sometimes a hanging mist clouding and softening the hills in a white wrap. At others, a dense wall of sheeting water. The car park is churned up, islands of pale mud in pools of brown water.

Ted has bought a car. A black shiny Range Rover with windows tinted so dark it is impossible to see inside. A car for the upper middle classes. A prestige vehicle. A four-wheel drive for the shopping set. A vehicle in which to roam the world. And how did a stinking old miser who can't drive make such a purchase? He paid cash — chose the vehicle from the showroom floor, and told the salesman to drive him home.

The power of money. No plastic, no cheque, no deposit and no payments. Cash. The full amount from the pocket of his dirty old trousers. The money was probably the cleanest thing on him. I have a twinge of anxiety. A touch of paranoia. Helping is one thing, getting caught is another. The number plates are shiny, black and white. A stray sunbeam, lonely in the clouds strikes off them.

"Whose name is it registered in, Ted?"

I get a shifty look from under those demented brows.

"Never you mind. They'll never find it."

This black high-rise vehicle with its aerials, wide tyres and new towbar is parked next to my old pickup. Guilt by association. Why didn't you park it down the other end of the carpark, you silly old fuck?

There is nothing to be gained by standing here idle. Action! We load our gear. Killing requires equipment. Especially the kind that Ted has in mind. Ropes, blankets, a thermos of coffee. Rosie tracks mud and water onto the pristine cloth of the back seat.

We have a job to do, a task to complete. I have fed and watered the animals and set the yeasts. We have forty-eight hours to find a man neither of us has ever seen.

But we know where he is. This secretive old bastard has been hiding the letter. Upon his person. Through the grime and the creases the words are still there. A letter from the killer to the victim. Asking for help, asking for money, claiming blood ties and kinship as justification for begging. The nephew wanted money. Lots of money for a scheme. A surefire unlosable, guaranteed trillion dollar return scheme. Or so he said. A letter with an address on it. Oh, how foolish, how thoughtless and unplanned.

We scramble up into the car, Ted a bit slower. He is still thin and gaunt but his colour is much improved. Or maybe it's because today he is clean. And pressed. Under his parka he is dressed to fit in. Maybe the task ahead permits the grieving to ease.

We're off to join the mid-week commuters. Rosie stretches out spreading the dirt a little further. It gives off a fine noise, this shiny black car. A genuine V8 burble. Ah, yes. This is a fine tool for a killing. And a killing can be a fine thing with the right music. How far have I come in these few weeks?

We swing out past the marina, past Sandy's pathetic little house where the new police tape flutters over the old, and begin the long climb up the hill towards the city. We turn, the two of us, hunters, our noses to the wind. We go south to that stinking seething mass of ignorance and pulchricide. Like all good hunters, we will assume the colours of the prey.

Ted is a man. He wants revenge. I am a woman. I am just tidying up.

We plunge into the sewer, this living stream of traffic and people, harried and aggressive. Ted is finding the journey difficult. At every traffic light he shrinks further into his seat. His glances out the black windows are furtive and nervous. Not that we excite any attention. We pass several four-wheel drives just like this one. The same model and colour. None with windows quite as dark. But who cares or even notices? In this weather the drivers have their shoulders hunched, a tunnel of vision which peers through the rain straight ahead. Pushing in and out of lanes, darting in front then falling behind. It is a long time since I have driven this deep into the city. I have forgotten it. I stay on the same road and presume it will lead us to where we want to go. And it does.

There in front of us rises the Centre. Buildings piled on top of each other like rats in a nest. Through occasional breaks in the cloud the tops of the high-rises peep through. Ted has a brief moment of panic when we get to the bridge. We have forgotten the toll and he fumbles for the coins. We are faced with the choice of over or under. Over the top on the bridge in the rain or underneath in the tunnel with the hiss of wet tyres. This is not a river like mine, wild and huge. This is a harbour neat and tamed. We go under for the novelty of the thing.

It is not so impressive a house, this 24 Fitzroy Crescent, Surry Hills. A white two-storey semi-detached. An attached neighbour on one side and a narrow driveway on the other. The yard is hidden behind a paling fence that needs attention. A tiny front yard with two terracotta pots home to a pair of poorly pruned cumquats.

How can these people live so close to the street? Strangers passing within metres, only the walls, mental and physical, to afford some fragile protection. Every sound, every movement belongs to every passerby, every disinterested neighbour. Young plane trees are planted in mean holes in the asphalt. They are tied to stakes with strips of hessian. Urban beautification. Like some grotesque gesture of defiance. Torture a tree and green your suburb.

No one is home. A sharp knock on the front door produces nothing but an echo. Ted is looking more and more furtive. Hang on, old man, we have a job to do here. The three of us walk down the side and around the back.

Well, well, well. What do we have here. A discovery. And what a discovery it is. All shiny and blue. Metal flake-blue, with lime-green flames spewing forth from the exhausts. The seats are padded royal blue velour. The floor is carpeted in green and blue. A boat such as this should be in a fair, a freak show. Or quietly sunk. The bung has not been removed and there are several inches of dirty water building up in the bilges.

We stand and stare, open mouthed and wondering. What else can we do? So this is what Jane was looking for. Does she knows it's here?

The back of the house has a small wooden deck running out from the kitchen and into a garden. Well, more a patch of neglect really. A wilderness. Bushy natives, tall weeds and a great deal of ivy on the wall between here and the neighbours. All of it dripping.

We go back to the car, settle down and wait with the endless patience and dedication of the serious hunter. My knife is on my hip and my heart is still. And so it will stay. Rosie climbs across from the back seat and nearly pushes Ted out the door so she can share his seat. She is half on the central console and half on him. He doesn't seem to mind.

We will wait. There is nothing else to do. We will wait and he will come. The nephew, the writer of the importunate letter.

The little house between the railway lines and the road hasn't changed. There are two patrol cars and an unmarked. The same condescending uniforms and the same bulky detectives. Dennis Turnbull and offsider. The only difference is the victim.

The pool of brown blood is enormous. It has flowed down the front of him, across his thighs and to the floor. His reading material is soaked.

"Guess he was a bit distracted. Never saw whoever came up behind him. What a way to go, eh. Wanking his heart out."

Turnbull is entertained.

For a moment I think Masterson's penis is missing and then realise that it has just shrunken inside his hand.

There is the sound of another car. Two figures in white overalls appear at the back door. Physical Evidence. They click open their cases and start working.

Cameron and I retire to the backyard. I can feel her thinking. But she says it anyway.

"Good riddance to bad rubbish, eh boss."

"Don't call me boss."

"No, ma'am. All the same, I can't help thinking someone has done us a favour. It's not like the local community is going to miss him or anything."

The local community. An orange utility pulls up with a roar. It is dusty and battered, a pair of mongrel dogs wearing studded collars in the back. The occupant, bearded, unkempt and reeking of fish, surges up the driveway.

He grabs the first uniform he sees and starts yelling.

"Who did this, eh! Who did this? Who killed my mate? You bloody cops, I bet you did it. You gonna get them, then? Who did this? You gonna get them!"

The officer disengages himself and Dennis Turnbull comes out to see what the commotion is.

"Hang on, mate. What's the problem?"

"The problem! My best mate's just been killed, you fucking dickhead. And who did it, eh? It was youse wasn't it? You bloody did me mate."

"Calm down and don't be stupid. Of course we didn't kill him. Jesus, you stink."

This last seems to have some impact. He hangs his head and shuffles a bit.

"Yeah, well. I been out in the boat, eh. Sorry, eh. I'm just a bit upset. He was me mate."

Turnbull looks over to me, a question in his glance. I nod and he takes his malodorous companion by the arm.

"Come on, mate. Come and talk to the Chief Inspector here. She'll be handling this case."

Masterson's mate doesn't like this.

"A sheila? A fucking sheila? You telling me that a sheila is supposed to find who did this?"

He smells like a hundred years of dead fish lying in a hot sun. It is difficult standing near him. This is going to be short.

"Is there anything you can tell us about this? When did you last see Masterson?"

"I don't have to talk to you. Who the hell are you?"

He moves as though to turn away but Cameron has slipped behind him, cutting off his line of retreat. He gives a despairing look at Turnbull who is headed back to the house.

"I am Detective Chief Inspector Stewart and I am the head of Homicide for this region. If you want us to find out who killed your friend then you will most definitely have to talk to me. When did you last see him?"

He's all bluff.

"Well, we had a few drinks last night to celebrate, eh. Him being out like. But I had to go. The tide was coming in and I had to get me traps set."

"Did you drink here?"

"Nah. Down the pub."

"What time did you leave him?"

"About ten, eh. There was still jokers with him when I left."

"Give your name and phone number to the sergeant. And don't go around saying that the police kill people. I don't like it."

"Ah, no miss."

Even wife killers have mates.

All I can think of is a figure standing on the hill behind me. Staring down at the body of Sandy Masterson. Wearing a white singlet.

On the drive back I tell Cameron the case is hers. She is not pleased.

"You don't get your choice of victims, sergeant. Check her family and his. And all their friends. Find out where every single one of them was last night."

Am I misleading her?

“There’s someone else watching your house.”

Fargo is delivering his report.

“There’s been a black Range Rover parked there for the last two days. Female driver, male passenger and a big dog. Car is registered to a company called EF Black, offices in Lindgard Street.”

“Anyone else?”

“Nope. And the occupants of the house seem to be away. It’s been empty since we’ve been watching.”

“Coburn?”

“Nothing suspicious. When he hasn’t been here he’s been working on that burning at Chatswood. Drove through Darlinghurst yesterday which seemed out of his way. Went on into Surry Hills and passed the turnoff to Fitzroy Crescent but didn’t stop anywhere.”

“Thanks. Keep it up.”

Ted is snoring. He and Rosie are a syncopated chorus. I feel the back of my neck prickle just before the back door opens and the grey eyes of my love fill the rear vision mirror.

"What do you think you are doing?"

She doesn't look happy. Ted jerks awake and Rosie turns round to slobber on the strong arm of the law. I am at something of a loss to explain our presence here.

"Pack up whatever little cockeyed scheme you have and go home. And you, Mr Jones, are inches away from being charged with obstruction. If either of you come anywhere near this place again you will both be arrested."

She slips out as quietly as she came.

Fancy that. The object of my devotion so near and I didn't even know. It must be the urban environment, my senses are all out of whack. I feel guilty. Damn it. I hate that. I have tried very hard to avoid the nasty tendrils of guilt and anxiety in my adult life and now here they come. Sneaking in the back door like that. This bit wasn't in the plan. Now what, eh. Shit.

My partner in crime looks suitably disgruntled. He sniffs and mutters to himself. I push Rosie into the back seat and start the car. We drive home, down but not out. There is a determined edge to Ted's snufflings.

Sean and Danelli's absence troubles me. I don't like it when suspects disappear. I wonder about Coburn, whether he knows where they are. And Matthews, a man for whom I have always had some respect.

I drive past his house. He lives in an Inner West suburb, not too classy, not too plain. The house is brick, solid and suburban. Is it larger than it should be? Are there hidden riches inside, marble skirting boards and gold taps? From the street I can see only a well-cared-for garden in conservative and predictable tastes. I don't know the names of the plants but they are the same as those cultivated by the neighbours. Nothing distinctive, nothing unusual. I toy with the idea of knocking on the door and talking to his wife but I have no explanation for my presence. I can do better work from my office.

When I get there Coburn is sitting at his desk typing. His head is bent away from me and he doesn't look up as I pass.

There is mail on my desk. As I flick through it one envelope falls out. It is small, white and marked "personal". Inside is one sheet of paper with no return address.

"Keep your nose clean, dyke bitch, or we'll clean it for you."

The font is Times, 14 point and it appears to come from a laser printer. I have a file of threats and offensive letters collected over the years. This is the first in a few months. I give it a fresh folder, mark the date and put it with the others.

Movement catches the corner of my eye through the tinted glass and the door opens. Matthews comes in. Hearty and avuncular.

"How goes it, Jane? Nose to the grindstone, eh."

"Sir."

What's he doing here? This is my turf.

"How's this Porter killing going? You know it's an interesting case that one. This connection back to Steve Danelli. I remember him. We were chasing him back in the old Darlo days. Never found anything though."

A million suspicions start flooding through my mind. I have yet to include Danelli in my reports. He hooks a chair with his foot, pulls it closer and sits down. I concentrate on relaxing my face.

"Do you remember a senior called Mick Chambers, sir? From that time?"

"Oh yes, there was always something dodgy about Mick. Lots of rumours but I always found him to be a good cop myself. Took stress leave and died a few years back. Swimming or something."

His body is quite relaxed, nothing special in his face. A man at ease. My assessment of Chief Superintendent Matthews may well have been erroneous. I wait. So does he and as the silence stretches I begin to feel his anxiety. There isn't much but it's there. Matthews is worried about something. He breaks first; after all, he has come to my office, uninvited.

"Leave, Jane. You haven't taken any for nearly twenty-four months. You should give some serious thought to it. Even the best of us burn out, you know."

He leans forward slightly, warmth and concern beaming from his round face. He has nothing but my best interests at heart.

"I thought I would take some in a couple of months, sir."

"Excellent. Very good."

That's it. He leaves. Through the glass I can see Coburn watching.

"They're back."

Fargo drops his reports on the desk.

"The occupants of 24 Fitzroy Crescent returned this morning at 11.48. They appeared to have been holidaying. They unpacked several suitcases from the back of a yellow BMW, were both very tanned, talking and laughing. They are still there."

I swivel my chair. Coburn is at his desk, diligently working.

If I pull Sean and Danelli now I will blow Coburn. Waiting, again.

"I want to know the instant Coburn goes anywhere near them."

RIVER'S EDGE

PART FOUR

Valentine

We have a new plan, Ted and I. A subtle, seductive ploy to get our two city boys into our clutches. A letter. So simple, so easy. So appropriate. Ted writes to Sean and tells him that Ryan had a will.

Oh yes. Greed will win out every time. A sweet letter all innocence and charm. We send it off and we sit and wait. We have made preparations and the day will come.

Life continues. The rhythms of baking and weeding, baking and planting, beat on. The chef boy likes his bunnies. I don't like him. He pesters me for more, lying in wait when I make my deliveries to the marina. I am forced, by his persistence, to be rude. He doesn't take it well.

Ted clutches the prospect of revenge to his scrawny bosom and cleans up his garden. He takes Rosie hunting and a bloody marsupial carcass hangs from the hooks in his ceiling. The shiny black car slowly turns grey with dust and mud over in the car park. When I ask what he is going to do with it Ted mutters and turns away.

My girl visits.

There are times, as we lie in the sun, golden and naked, when I can feel her watching me. I can feel her instincts and intuitions probing and poking below the surface of our desire and wonder what conclusions she has reached. She tells me that sweet Sergeant Alice Cameron is in charge of the Masterson killing and I wonder why she did so.

She gives me the keys to her home. A place I have never seen in a city I avoid. I never thought about visiting her. She always seems so happy to come here. For me to go there, away from the river, it would be something ... I don't know but I quail at the thought. Her courage is greater then mine.

But I can forget all this so easily in the slope of her thigh and the scent of her neck. I put her in my kayak and teach her to paddle across the bright sunny water. She tells me, tense and nervous, that she is frightened of water. I always laugh when she tells me this. My swimmer who is afraid of the water. But this seems to make her try harder, pushes her forward with effort. She does not retreat. The river washes Masterson's blood away and I dream about a future for us.

On a perfect summer Tuesday the letter is answered. I have just finished my deliveries and my island squats before me when I see it. It comes from the marina to starboard, roaring, stinking and bouncing across the chop. *Phantasy*, metal flake blue with green flames. A vile and horrible boat carrying thieves and deceivers. They have come, as we knew they would. What thief could resist? Two empty heads, hair chaotic in the wind. They don't even see me.

As they roar, heedless and stupid, up Ted and Ryan's creek, I drop the dogs off at my wharf and exchange boats. This job calls for a shallow draught. My knife is on my hip. I slip upstream, past the entrance to the creek and along beneath the river cliffs. The rendezvous is already set.

It is mid afternoon before I see the Halverson. She glides through the water with almost no wake and no noise. A lovely smooth passage. The *Annie Marie* is a boat of great beauty. A fine craft for a noble deed. A killing can be a fine thing with the right music.

Ted brings her in close to the cliffs and drops the anchor with a rattle of chain. From my alcove in the rocks, hidden by an overhanging blackbutt, I can see Ted, the nephew and the boyfriend standing on the aft deck. Ted goes down the companionway to the saloon and they follow.

I paddle across to the launch and around to the rear platform. I slip the kayak's painter over a cleat on the gunwale and move from my boat to his. Quietly, quietly, secret and sure. Across the deck and stop beside the companionway. I can hear their voices.

Ted is telling the nephew that Ryan has left him the boat. His old thin voice is monotone, arrhythmic as he weaves the boy about with lies.

"Ryan wanted you to have this. It was important to him. After he got your letter we talked about selling it, giving you the money. We're too old now. What do we need it for, a big boat like this. It's worth a bit, ya know."

Then a deeper voice, strong and sceptical.

"Why didn't he tell us this? If we had known, we would have come to see him before he died."

"Yeah. I always wanted to meet Uncle Ryan. My Mum used to talk about him. How he was such a good guy and gay and everything."

Liars and deceivers. Do they think we are so foolish?

The strong voice again.

"How much is a boat like this worth? Real estate is more my thing. Boats ... I'd have to get advice on it."

"If we sell it, Steve. After all, Uncle Ryan's memory and everything. It might be more respectful to keep it."

I hear a cupboard door slide back and the clink of glass. Ted's voice asks if anyone wants a drink. He doesn't have to do it twice.

How can they do this, this evil pair, pretend? Take the hospitality of the lover and deny the killing of the loved. How can they do this?

I close the hatch behind me as I walk down the steps to join them. The two thieves look up startled. The older one, the boyfriend, is closest to me. I step up to him and take the glass from his hand. He tries to grab for it and the whisky spills, acrid and smoky in the closed air. It is all so simple. I knee him in the groin, very hard and he goes down like a falling rock. Spittle foams at his mouth and he struggles to breathe. His face is absolutely white, startled, disbelieving, brown eyes bulging.

The nephew drops his glass and jumps back.

"What the ..."

He turns towards Ted and straight into the barrel of Ryan's old bolt action 303. A good gun, steadfast and reliable. Nothing fancy, nothing modern. Even killing has its classics. Ted pushes him back onto the bunk that runs along the side of the cabin. He stays there transfixed and immobile, enslaved by the hole at the end of the barrel.

The man on the floor is beginning, slowly, to recover. Before he gets much further I have his arms behind his back and his wrists tied. I firmly (very firmly) wrap four metres of nylon triple twist 11 mm rope around his upper body. He is mine — or ours — or anybody's in this state. He can move his legs but that is all. He doesn't seem to want to straighten them at this point anyway. He is still having trouble with his breathing.

The nephew looks most apprehensive as I turn towards him.

"Who the fuck are you? What's going on? Jesus, Ted, what do you think you're doing? We haven't done ... we didn't. No, no. Don't touch me. Christ, what's wrong with you people?"

I have to hit him to shut him up. He gets the same treatment as his buddy. They look almost comfortable wrapped up in their warm cocoons of clean, fresh, yellow and white rope. Almost pretty against the teal blue carpet of the saloon's deck.

Except for their faces. Fear seems to be a new experience for both of them.

Ted puts down the rifle and gags them with strips torn from an old pair of pyjamas. Dirty ones from the victims' expressions. I go back out to the sunshine.

This stretch of the river is invariably deserted. The *Annie Marie* is the only vessel in sight. The cliffs are turning deep red in the glow from the afternoon sun.

The nephew's head appears up the steps with Ted and gun behind him. He has difficulty keeping his balance. Ted pushes him out onto the rear platform. I slide into my kayak and slip the painter. Ted kicks the boy in the back of the knees. He falls forward into the water his face a spasm of terror as he drops past me.

But he doesn't drown. I grab him as he goes by and haul him across the kayak's foredeck.

"If you keep still, you'll be alright. Wriggle and you'll fall off."

He takes my advice and lies across my deck like a shot seal. I paddle carefully back to the cliffs. Behind the overhanging blackbutt is the tiny entrance to a large pool. It is hidden, secret, dark with shadows. The wind and the water have scoured out the base of the cliff leaving a pool that is nearly four metres deep on a 1.4 high tide. In three hours the tide will be at 1.5.

I take the canoe into the pool and over to the base of the cliff. A ledge there stays dry on even the highest tide. I hoist my dying seal onto it and leave him there.

"Don't try and roll off. If you fall in you'll drown."

Pushing with his legs he wriggles his butt further up the rock leaving wet marks as he goes. His head keeps bobbing up and down. He is nodding as fast as he can go. Much more of that and his brain will shake loose.

I paddle back to the *Annie Marie*. Ted is waiting with the other one already on the platform. The man with the bruised balls is having trouble standing. His breathing is still irregular and only the rope seems to be holding him up. Ted doesn't have to kick his knees. He just lets him go and the man falls into the water. I struggle to get him onto the kayak. He is limp and heavier than his boyfriend.

Ted stows the rifle in the locker on the rear deck and slips into the water beside me, a blue garbage bag in his hand. He swims beside my boat as we splash back to the pool. He climbs onto the ledge while I wait, my burden dripping and flaccid. The nephew can't decide whether to move or stay still. Ted solves his dilemma. As the boy flaps his legs, Ted turns and kicks him hard in the thigh. It is a concentrated and determined kick, vicious and angry.

The sheltering blackbutt has an aberrant arm stretched across the pool about three metres from the water's surface. From his plastic bag, Ted pulls more rope. He carefully and slowly separates it into two lengths about ten metres each. He coils one, stands, and with a smooth and practised flick of his aging wrist, sends the rope out and over the blackbutt's branch. One end drops down to me as he anchors the other on a ring bolt in the sandstone above the ledge.

I tie my end around the chest and under the arms of my man then slide him into the water. He hangs from the tree, the water just above his waist. He lifts his head and tries to look up above him. This seems to put some strain on the lower parts of his body and his neck spasms. He rolls his head sideways and looks straight at me. Behind the pain of his balls and the ropes, it's all there. He knows. He knows where he is, why he's there and what is going to happen.

I turn away to get the other one. Ted flicks the second rope out and the boy goes frantic. He starts kicking and pushing himself as far up the ledge as he can go. Behind the gag his face is stricken, white and contorted. A long wail reverberates across the pool.

I grab the rope and take the kayak into the ledge. I drop the painter across the branch of a Prickly Moses and slip out onto the rock. As I kick the boat away it swings and bobs as far from the fighting boy as I can make it.

Ted kicks him again but the boy won't stop moving. Ted lifts the end of the rope above his head and swings it down. He whips him across the shoulders, the face, the trunk. The boy wriggles faster, a demented snail as Ted whistles the rope through the air. When it hits the noise is soft and dull as if the boy's body is absorbing the sound. His moan has turned to a high pitched keening. The blood rushes to his face as he tries to get more air through the gag. There are deep red welts erupting on his skin. The rope end cuts his cheek open and the blood stains the nylon. Blood stripes appear on his shoulders and chest as Ted keeps hitting him.

I wrap my arms around Ted from behind and pull him back. His arms flail the air. I squeeze until he can't breath properly. Then all the anger leaves and he relaxes in my hold. He shakes his head and mumbles.

"I'm alright. Lemme go."

I do and his legs crumple. He sinks down onto the stone and curls his knees to his chest.

I don't like the beating. A killing, a death — that I know and understand. But to beat something, someone. I have no stomach for that. I know why Ted did it. The howling emptiness inside him is as plain as the bloodstained rope in his hand. But a beating is sour, as vicious and mean as the two we're here to judge.

I sink down beside Ted. Above me the sun is setting and the cliff is the colour of the boy's face. My ears are ringing with his crying. It is shrill and high, one note repeated over and over, bounced and amplified by the rocks. It fills the air like something solid. His face is starting to turn blue under the blood. He is struggling to breathe but still he cries.

Before I can move Ted is up and over him. His foot crunches across the boy's throat. The bound body spasms, legs out rigid and quivering. His back arches and the blood vessels break in his eyes. The sound stops. Ted has crushed his windpipe. Already starved of oxygen he dies quite quickly, his face bulging and blue. Ted stands above him and watches, relaxed and curious, a gardener admiring a new variety.

Ted comes when I pull his arm. He sits under the shelter of the cliff and stares out to the man hanging from the tree in the fading light. The tide is rising. It is up to the man's chest.

I undo the ropes from the boy's body and return him to the deck of the kayak. I edge the boat back out into the river and across to the *Annie Marie*. It is something of a struggle to get the boy onto the platform but I manage it. I drag him back into the saloon and dump him, wet and bloody, on the carpet. His pants are wet and soiled with piss, shit and river.

By the time I get back to Ted and our second victim it is almost dark. As I come across the pool he turns his head toward me in the shadow and tilts his chin, beckoning. When I come up to him he pushes the gag towards me. I lean over and cut it from him. He spits and it falls, a rag in the water. The tide is just above his armpits.

Ted watches from the ledge. The man turns to him, his voice weak now and resigned.

"I know why you are doing this but we never meant to kill him. The old man. I didn't even know he existed until Sean decided to write to him. I've been having trouble, you see. Money. Of course, what else, eh. There is a man, he's been putting the pressure on. I owe him. Well, he says I do. They had Sean beaten up a few times. We just needed the money but the old man … Ryan … he wouldn't. He just laughed at Sean and told him he was a fool. It wasn't my fault. I didn't do it. Sean hit him with the spanner. Please …"

The words come out slow and wheezy as if it hurts him to speak. The ropes must be constricting his chest.

Ted just sits, a shape in the darkness.

"Sean … Sean … Oh Christ. How could you just … ? Could you … could you just shoot me? You've got that gun. Please. I don't want to just wait. That's what you're doing, aren't you? You're waiting for the tide to come in and drown me. But the old man — Ryan — we didn't drown him. He was already dead when Sean pushed him off the boat. Please. Just shoot me, please."

Ted doesn't move. I pull the man out of the water and onto my boat. I cut the rope hanging from the tree. I cut the rope around his body. He slips back into the water and hangs onto the life lines that run along the hull.

"Grab the toggle at the back of the boat and don't let go."

He does as I tell him. I turn the kayak, awkward in the restricted space of the pool, and paddle back out to the river. He hangs on all the way past the *Annie Marie* and back down to Porters Creek.

At Ted and Ryan's wharf *Phantasy* sits rocking gently in the darkness. I come in alongside it and tie up. I have to drag the exhausted man from the river. He is hypothermic. In the blue boat there are towels and a dry wet suit. I strip him off and rub him down. The shaking stops enough for him to struggle into the wet suit alone.

"Go back. Put your horrible boat on its trailer and never ever come back here. Whoever it is that frightens you, they are nothing compared to Ted. For you he is the angel of death. What he did to Sean he will do to you."

The stupid boat has no navigation lights. He takes it down the stream slowly, the water bubbling under the stern. The night is absolutely black.

I go home. The river demands a high price for its treasures.

Stewart

"Danelli is still there but Porter seems to have disappeared."

"What happened to the watchers?"

Fargo is embarrassed.

"Sorry, boss. Seems one of them is quite fond of golf. Well, there's no budget for this and so he took yesterday off. The boat's been moved too. It's parked in the street and still hitched to the car."

"Coburn?"

"Nothing suspicious so far."

"Watch him. If Porter has disappeared he will either know where he is or want to."

"No worries, boss. And I'm sorry about …"

He has the grace to look apologetic as he leaves. But he's right. This is a job on the side and who can blame his watchers for not caring that much?

I keep seeing Valentine and Ryan sitting outside Danelli's house. Masterson's throat gaping at his ceiling. But I can't ask. No matter how much I want to know, I can't break it, this fragile thing she has given me. I am in love and I am afraid.

I have received four more of the "dyke bitch" letters since the first. They are becoming more strident in tone. The last threatens me with dismemberment.

Cameron wants to talk. Out of the office. Something is troubling her. We meet at the end of a headland on the harbour. Two rowing clubs sit adjacent to a small park. One is on top of the headland and commands an expansive view. It is a large building with picture windows and a car park the size of two housing blocks. The other is the size of a small garage and perched below the slope on the edge of the children's playground.

The neon sign on the big one just says "Rowing Club". The paint on the side of the small one says "Women's Rowing Club". Cameron gives the big one a filthy look but doesn't comment. We sit on a bench by the swings. The weather has been hot and clear for days. The sky is pale with the city and the water sparkles. I can feel the edges of the flaking paint on the bench through the thin linen of my pants. Cameron is having trouble getting started.

"I was interviewed by IAD last night, ma'am. About you."

"You shouldn't be telling me this, sergeant."

"No, ma'am. It was a Sergeant Ross. She was waiting for me when I got home. She wanted to know what your relationship was with Valentine. Whether I thought there was any cause for concern. She suggested that maybe there was something improper going on between you. I tried to find out who had made a complaint but she wouldn't say."

She fiddles with her car keys, flicking them back and forth across her fingers like a set of worry beads.

"It's this business about Mick Chambers too, ma'am. Chambers and Danelli. It worries me. A cop and a suspected dealer in business together. Anyway, I've been asking around, quietly, and it seems Chambers was an old friend of Mick Coburn's."

There's a long pause. I wait.

"And Danelli? Well, he's definitely smelly. I mean, we're looking at him for the Porter killing and he just doesn't seem to have any visible means of support. His tax return says he earned less than twenty thousand last year."

She moves, uncomfortable on the bench, but stays seated. She watches some gulls fight over a garbage bin, then continues.

"I found the letting company for those apartments Danelli owns. They wouldn't tell me much but they did say which bank they deposit the rents into. The manager there told me even less at first but she was a woman and I don't think she liked the idea of maybe holding a drug dealer's accounts."

At this point she smirks.

"I'd also met her before. She, ah, isn't married."

She shoots a sidelong glance my way to see what I make of this.

"Anyway, she says that Danelli's account seems to be a holding facility. The money goes out almost as soon as it goes in. And it's usually withdrawn in cash. Over the counter. It's a small branch and she can see the tellers from her desk. The same man collects the money every time. I showed her some photographs of Danelli and Porter from the old Darlo files. She didn't recognise them but she did pick out another one I showed her."

There's a long pause. She wriggles some more.

"It was Coburn, ma'am. He's a signatory on the account."

The gulls engage in a minor skirmish and we both watch as though we have all the time in the world.

"IAD have investigated Coburn twice, sergeant, and found nothing."

"Yes, ma'am, I know."

"Why did you just happen to have Coburn's picture with you?"

"I had a selection, ma'am. I even showed her yours. She didn't know you."

I don't comment. She is troubled enough.

"Don't forget the Masterson case, Alice. You may not like him but he's still yours."

I have a meeting with my peers. Once a week the heads of each section brief each other on major cases. Around the conference table on Matthews' floor we sit, Homicide, Armed Hold Ups, Drugs, Child Protection and Break Ins. Car Thefts is on leave. I am the only woman. Matthews presides like a generous uncle.

Everything is routine until we are leaving. Matthews gestures for me to stay. He gives me the spiel about leave again, about taking care of myself, my stress levels. I hear the others get in the lift and the doors closing.

When I get away, Charlie Black is waiting by the lift doors. He is a tall man, as tall as I am. He took over Drugs in this region when Matthews became Regional Commander.

In the lift he pushes the button for my floor and smiles at me.

"Glorious weather we've been having, Jane."

I don't respond.

"Wonderful things you've been doing with Homicide, you know. Ray was just saying the other day, there's a fine career path ahead of you, Jane. A fine one. An example to us all."

Then he turns towards me, holds my gaze.

"It would be a pity to make a mistake at this point, wouldn't it, my dear. After all, we all know how hard it is for someone like you. The whispers, the innuendo. You need friends, people who will look out for you."

We arrive and the doors sigh open. I step out as he reaches for the button and holds the lift.

"Ray's a good man, Jane. He's got a lot of friends in the Service."

The doors close then and he disappears.

Coburn is sitting at his desk. He has hardly been out of the building in the past couple of weeks. This is more likely to be Matthews' idea than his own.

I wonder if Matthews knows about the Danelli bank account. It seems too stupid a thing for him. But then again, sometimes even the smart ones overlook the obvious. Today I am counting on Coburn's apparent diligence.

Nguyen and Orr can't keep the swagger out of their walks. They strut in from the foyer, Danelli between them. He looks pale, stressed, older than his forty odd years. The three men walk past Coburn's desk, each looking straight ahead.

They come into my office and Orr pushes Danelli into a chair. Nguyen leans against the wall by the door he has just closed. Danelli sits passive and resigned. His eyes stay locked on my desk top.

"Thank you for coming in, Mr Danelli. I am Chief Inspector Stewart and I am conducting an investigation into the death of Ryan Porter. Would you like a cup of coffee? Sam."

As Nguyen leaves the room I turn and see Coburn leave his desk. He goes out to the foyer and Fargo follows him.

"Did you know Ryan Porter, Mr Danelli?"

"No."

"So you have never met him."

"No."

"Are you sure of that?"

"Yes, I'm sure."

"Where's Sean?"

"What?"

This time his eyes come up and he looks at me.

"Where is Sean?"

"Gone. He's ... just gone."

"Left you?"

He swivels his head as Nguyen returns with coffee, milk and sugar on a tray. Very nice, Sam.

Danelli looks from him to Orr, assessing. He ignores the tray in front of him.

"Yes, he's left me."

"Why?"

"I don't see what that has to do with anything."

He leans forward and pours milk into the cup, then stirs in two spoons of sugar. He does it slowly, a distraction. He takes a drink, a healthy swallow. Steam rises from the coffee but he doesn't seem to notice the heat.

"Mr Danelli, let me explain. Ryan Porter was Sean Porter's uncle. We know that you and Sean are in need of money. Ryan Porter has more money than you have ever dreamed of. We know that two men answering your descriptions were in your boat on the river on or around the day that Ryan Porter was killed. This was extremely unusual. Ryan was a hermit. He did not get visits from his family. Perhaps you can clarify this for us."

He stares at the coffee. Something is wrong here. For one moment I think he is going to cry but then it passes and he is under control again.

"No, I can't help you."

"You don't get the rent from the buildings you own, do you?"

That gets his attention.

"I don't know what you're talking about."

"Why are you broke? Those two buildings each return around $8000 a week but you don't have it. Even your tax return says you're broke. Where does your money go, Mr Danelli? Who gets it?"

"Are you arresting me?'

"No, I'm not arresting you."

"I can go then."

"Yes, you can go."

He gets up slowly. More than anything, this man is tired, exhausted. I try again.

"Steve, if I'm right in what I think has happened to Sean, I may well be your safest option. And if Sean killed Ryan, by mistake maybe, or in anger, that doesn't mean you have to go down for it."

He shakes his head and makes a sound, part sob, part laugh. Then he's up and out the door. Nguyen follows him to the foyer.

"Jamie, you and Sam stick to him like glue. If Mick Coburn comes anywhere near him I want to know immediately."

"Yes, boss."

He practically flies after his colleague.

"And don't call me boss."

The dogs hear me before I get there. They bark and carry on, sniffing and rubbing. The light spills out across the gardens. The glass doors are open and she is sitting inside at the kitchen table. A beer bottle with no label sits in front of her. It is nearly empty.

She doesn't move or acknowledge my presence. There is no welcome. She rubs her hand through her hair and, for the first time since I have loved her, she looks smaller, shrunken. When she speaks her voice is dull, despairing.

"There's not much point your coming. I can't tell you what you want to know."

"I'm not after you and Ted. I've got my suspicions about what you've done but you're not the main game here. I need to know what Steve Danelli told you. What happened. I know he has been up here, on the river."

She looks away.

"Sean's missing but it's not him I'm after. Yes, I know he probably killed Ryan but it's Danelli I need. I need to know his connections. I know he was up here. What happened?"

"I can't help you."

"Dammit, Valentine, I am so involved with you it scares the hell out of me. If you and Ted have done what I think you have I'm out. My career is so far over the line I'm hanging in space. There is a high ranking officer in this, a bad one. He's very clever and he's well protected. I need your help."

She drops her head into her hands One of the dogs pushes against her arm. She leans back in the chair and looks up at me. Her eyes are wet, they gleam in the light.

"I can't help you, Jane. I'm sorry. This ... this is my world here. I don't understand anything else."

We don't even touch.

It seems to take forever to get back down the hill to the water. I keep stumbling in the darkness. When I get there the tide has come up higher and my little boat is wedged under the wharf. I struggle to get it free. I use an oar to lever it out from under and slip in the dark. I knock my hand against one of the uprights and feel the old oyster shells cut through my knuckles. Blood drips down my wrist.

The boat pops out and bobs in the current. I want to stay there. I want to rush back up that hill and tell her I don't care what she's done. I want to wrap myself around her and stay here forever, safe and sheltered.

The engine starts on the first pull and I drive away from her. The blackness is absolute, no horizon, no shoreline. I have only the vaguest notion of where to point this tiny tin boat. Then as I come out of the shadow of the island I see the marina lights across the river, a beacon, the entrance back to my world, away from this damn river.

The phone is ringing in the car. I can hear it as soon as I bounce across the waves into the marina. By the time I have tied the boat to its berth the phone has stopped then started again.

It's Orr. He's hysterical.

"Boss, oh shit boss, you've gotta get up here. Sam's dead. They've killed Sam."

"Jamie, slow down. Where are you?"

"Fitzroy Crescent. I'm sorry."

I can feel him trying to get control.

"There was a bomb in Danelli's house. It went off about half an hour ago. You've gotta get here. The locals are trying to take over. Danelli was inside somewhere, God knows. Sam went for coffee. He was walking past when it blew. They've taken him to St Vincent's."

"Is Fargo there?"

"No boss. I haven't seen him."

"I'm coming, Jamie. You'll be alright. Just hang on a bit longer."

The street is red and gleaming. The lights from the fire trucks reflect and bounce across the water running across the tarmac. Danelli's house is gone. Just the back wall remains held up by one corner. It clings precariously to what had been its neighbour. The roof, the windows, the doors, the front walls are gone. The fire is out. Nothing is left to burn. Firemen are rolling hoses and one is sweeping broken glass into the gutter. Glass lies everywhere, gleaming in the lights. The air is hot and steamy, thick with smoke.

Three broadcasting trucks have claimed a section of the pavement but no one is filming. The exciting bits are over.

Orr is a dark shape on the edge of the redness. I touch him on the shoulder and he nearly collapses against me. His face is grimy, white streaks running down his cheeks. I put him in my car and leave him.

Bill Roberts is the local Patrol Commander and he is talking to the Fire Station Officer. When he sees me he comes over. We have met before. Roberts is old style but pragmatic. He won't want this.

"Bill. What's the story?"

"A bomb, ma'am, and a big one. This used to be a two-storey house. I understand from your boy that there was someone inside. The fireys haven't found anything but ... well, you can see for yourself. There wouldn't be much left."

"Neighbours?"

"Not home, thank God. One of your boys was out the front. They've taken him to St Vinnies. He's alive but only just. This was an operation of yours, ma'am?"

He's unhappy. No Commander likes other operations on their patch. Especially dirty ones they don't know about.

"Not really, Bill. It was just someone we were watching."

"Well, if there was someone inside it's a homicide."

He says this quite hopefully. If it's homicide it's mine and he can wash his hands of it.

"Don't worry, Inspector. This one is ours."

The Station Officer says the bomb was in the bedroom on the second floor and appears to have been plastic explosive. He tells me, aggressively, that they won't know anymore for a few days. The fireys distrust and dislike us, usually with good reason. Arson are coming to have a look when it cools down.

I leave Orr at the hospital. Nguyen is in theatre. He is still alive.

Fargo is not answering his phone. I send and resend all the way back to my flat. Nothing. I hope he's been listening to his radio. As I pull down the lane that leads to the garage a dark blue Commodore comes in behind me. The security grill rolls up and the other car follows me in. It parks in the space next to mine. The garage is poorly lit and I am tired. I wait.

The door opens and the driver gets out.

"It's only me, boss."

Fargo slides into my passenger's seat.

"I didn't want to answer the phone. You never know who's listening and things are getting a little hot, eh."

"Was it Coburn?"

"Nope. Well, not directly. After Sam and Jamie brought Danelli into the office Mick hightailed it down to the street. He got a cab to the railway station. Then he made a phone call from one of the booths there. He kept the cab and took it to Matthews' house but he didn't go in. He just sat there for about five, seven minutes then had the cabbie take him to his place. He and Matthews live miles away from each other. It must have been some fare.

"Anyway, a couple of hours after he got home, his wife left in her car. I wasn't sure what to do then, whether to follow her and leave him or to stay. I think this story you're following goes back a good few years so I figured it's probably a family affair. I followed her to uni. I was going to give up on her, thought I'd made the wrong call, when she met someone. A girl, mid twenties and I've never seen her before but I tell ya, boss, she was a dead ringer for Matthews. Poor kid. Anyway, this kid gives Coburn's wife an attache case.

"Mrs Coburn doesn't hang around the uni, like, no classes or anything. She heads straight for Surry Hills. Goes to Danelli's place, heads around the back, comes out a minute later sans briefcase. Then drives back to hubby. You tell me who did it, boss."

"Was Danelli there when Mrs Coburn arrived?"

"Don't think so. I couldn't see Sam and Jamie on the street so I figure if they aren't there then neither is he. I never thought about a bomb, boss. I'm sorry. How's Sam?"

"Critical. They're moving fast, Tom."

"Yep. Coburn left the office mid morning. His wife had that briefcase within six hours. The bomb goes off just before ten. Danelli's dead within twelve hours of you talking to him and Porter is still missing. This is some organisation."

Fargo pulls out his Drum and rolls a smoke. He does it with one hand, so smooth it's almost a reflex. I turn the ignition on and drop his window. The smoke smells sour.

"Where are you going to take this, boss? I mean we don't have any real evidence of anything. You think Matthews and Coburn are connected, don't you? IAD have already cleared Coburn twice and Matthews ... ? What have you got against him? I saw someone I think is his daughter give Coburn's wife a briefcase. But I can't say what was in it or what she did with it. It's a classic, eh boss. All connections and conjecture. What about the Commissioner?"

"He and Matthews went through the Academy together. They still play golf on Thursday afternoons. Matthews' wife is his cousin."

We just sit there, the smoke from his rollie wafting out the window in the dim blue light.

"I had a visit from IAD a couple of days ago. They're after you.

Trying to dig something out of the Porter case. And if Sam dies Matthews will have a big say in who handles the inquiry. You don't have to worry about me, boss, but they'll make a case against you if he tells them to."

I think about the "dyke bitch" letters sitting in my office and wonder if my flat is empty.

"You could just close the file, have a drink and walk away."

"Is anyone watching Coburn?"

"Right now? Nope. You want me to come up with you?"

"No."

"Look, boss, he's going to kill you if he thinks you're going to be a problem. He'll send Coburn and Mick can be a very vicious boy. Why don't you let me hang around with you for a while. Just until all this settles down."

"We can talk about it later."

I get out of the car and so does he, slowly. I beep the alarm and walk across to the lift. He stands by his car and watches. As the lift door opens I turn.

"Thanks, Tom."

"No worries, boss."

The corridor outside my flat is empty. I put the key in the lock and I can feel my pulse racing. The blood is tingling in my fingertips and the oyster-shell cuts on my knuckles burst afresh. As I push the door open a blast of cold air chills me. Across the room the glass door to the tiny balcony is open. The curtain blows in the wind.

I do not, generally, carry a gun. I have one. It is locked in the gun safe in my office. I cannot remember if I shut the balcony door this morning or not. Up this high the street lights don't have much effect. I shut the door behind me and walk across the middle of the room. The furniture is sparse and there is little to hide behind. I close the balcony door and the wind drops.

The kitchen is tiny. A mouse couldn't hide in there. The bedroom is empty. The shower curtain gives me a brief moment of terror but the bathroom is clear. If there is anyone here they are very, very small. I strip off and fall into bed not bothering with the lights.

Valentine

It was not what I expected. No cleanliness, no surgical excision, no clarity. It was just bad. A great task gone rotten, putrid at the core.

I sit on the terrace and stare. This is my home, my safety, my refuge but today it is no help. Today is bad and perhaps, so am I. I am unused to regrets. Certainly ones of this magnitude. Ted's needs were not mine. The pit I willingly stepped into has become a mire of shame and diminishment. I am lessened.

Hanging them in the tide was to extract a confession. Which in one way it did. And then there was to be a bullet. And that's all. Hubris, arrogance. I believed I was in control. And now here I sit. I have lost my girl, I have judged my friend and found him wanting and I sink in a slough of my own despair. I have foundered in the swamp of cruelty. Masterson was quick and clean. Masterson was my job. This was Ted's.

As a child I watched my father whip a horse. He was a man of quick and violent temper and the poor beast had scraped his leg on a barbed wire fence. He had dismounted and holding the bridle with one arm he used his stock whip. The horse had screamed, frantic to escape, hauling back in a circle each time the whip came down. Great welts cut through the sweat and foam on its shoulders and flanks. He screamed with it each time he struck until the air was solid with sound. Eyes white with fear and pain, it reared so far back it lifted him off the ground and still he hit it. Across the legs, the belly, anywhere the whip would reach. It was a white horse. He turned it pink with the blood.

I have no hope that Danelli will be forgiving. Why should he be? If I was he I would go back to the city and scream from the tallest tree. I never thought that he might love the boy. I never thought. I never thought that Ted was the same as all men. But why should he not be? Why should I expect him to be different?

And if my love had been killed? Would I have done the same? But my love is dead. I have killed it myself. My girl is gone.

Enough of this melodrama. It is as despicable as my deed. Who am I to guard the river? The river guards itself. The dough must still be set. The water still flows.

I have checked. The *Annie Marie* is back in the lagoon and Ted is home. The body of Sean Porter? I have not asked.

Stewart

Sam Nguyen is dead. He died at 7.30 this morning. Orr, Fargo and Cameron are in my office. Beyond the darkened glass the other personnel are moving slowly, voices are muted, phones turned down.

On my desk lies another letter — "We got him, we'll get you, cunt." It didn't come in the mail. It was here waiting when I arrived.

It is some minutes since anyone has spoken. Orr is leaning against the wall by the door. He has adopted Sam's stance. Cameron speaks.

"Coburn's here."

Orr reaches for the door but before he can go through Fargo grabs him and swings him into the chair by my desk. I reach across and grab his arm.

"Jamie. We are still on this job. It is by no means over. If you go anywhere near Coburn it will blow any chance we have of clearing it up."

Under my hand his forearm is like wire, his whole body focused through the glass onto Coburn. Fargo grabs his hair and forces him to look at me.

"Constable, you will go out there and you will behave normally. You will have no dealings with Sergeant Coburn that are outside of your normal routine. Behave yourself or I will put you on stress leave immediately and you are out of this case. Do you hear me?"

"Ma'am."

Then the tension leaves him and he slumps against the desk.

"Sorry, boss. You're right. It's okay, I won't fuck up."

"Good. And that goes for the rest of you. You've all got more work than you need. Get out there and do it. Tom, you stay."

Cameron shepherds Orr out the door. She walks with him to his desk, always between him and Coburn. Tom slips into the chair vacated by Orr.

"What do you want, boss?"

Swinging around in my chair, I lean over to the gun safe behind my desk and open it. I slide my seldom used service revolver across the desk to Fargo and tell him what I want.

Superintendent Matthews is sitting at his desk. Before him is the morning's paper. Fitzroy Crescent is front page, more picture than story.

There are no details about Danelli or Nguyen. They say Sam is critical. He died too late for the presses.

I hand him my carefully worded report. The first report of my career with conscious and deliberate omissions.

"Terrible thing to lose such a fine young officer, Jane. Terrible thing. There will be an inquiry, of course."

He shakes his head, all concern and empathy.

"Very stressful for his mates and his commander. You need to take leave, Jane. You're a miracle worker but even you have to rest sometime."

He is a study in earnest compassion. I have sat in this chair in this office at least three times a week for the past eighteen months. I have spoken to this man hundreds of times. He is a superintendent, the Commander of the Regional Crime Squad. He's not some sly sergeant shaking down dealers in a back alley. This is a powerful and respected man. He is a confidant of the commissioner.

"And this Ryan Porter killing. No further on that are we? That woman, Valentine. You're sure we shouldn't be after her a bit more? Maybe protective custody is in order. Mick Coburn could take care of her."

I concentrate on breathing, slow and steady, in and out. Just sit there and look at him until the pain and the fear pass. They do and with them go my doubts.

"I don't believe that would be an appropriate course of action, sir."

He is fishing. He is unsure of what I know. He's pushing for a reaction. I give him one.

"I don't believe that Sergeant Coburn has much of a career left in this service."

He eases back in his chair. It creaks under the weight. The bonhomie and concern are gone like snow in a heatwave. His face is suddenly thinner, tight and hard. This, at last, is the real man. The one I never saw.

"Oh?"

"Mick Coburn is a corrupt thug, but he's not smart enough to run anything on his own."

The silence drags on for ever. He holds my gaze as I hold his. His voice, when it comes, is slow and measured. Colder than the words.

"You'd better have some evidence before you start throwing your weight around."

"Mick Coburn is your vulnerability. Old style coppers like him, not too bright, lazy, incompetent, are easily corrupted and they are easily broken. In the end, no matter what happens to me, you're not going to win. If I don't catch you someone else will."

As I walk away he slams his hand down on the desk. By the time I get back to my floor I am angry. With myself. I should have kept my mouth shut. All I've done is confirm his suspicions. These passions are too much for me.

Coburn spends the day at his desk. I seek refuge in routine. I read reports and understand nothing. I can't remember the sentence I have just finished. When I work on the computer the screen saver keeps coming on. My hands don't move on the keys.

The day finally ends. I stay until I am the last.

My footsteps echo across the empty garage. Fargo has left a gun and some shells in the glove box of my car. A throwdown with a silencer. No numbers. I sit in the passenger's seat and stare. I don't touch it. It lies there wrapped in oil paper, in the shadows among the old combs, coins, tampons and junk that always accumulates in a glove box. An anonymous death. Like most police officers in this city I have never killed. I have never fired a shot at another human being.

I want to go to the river, to the island, to Valentine. But there is no refuge there anymore. I start the car and drive to a small slightly grubby motel a few blocks from my flat. In a room with pale green walls and an orange carpet, I check the reception on my phone and replace the battery. Then I lie on the bed, turn on the TV and wait.

It's after midnight before I hear my phone. Three rings then it stops. I turn off the American hunk trying to sell me a home gym, swing my feet to the floor and walk out of a room I've barely touched.

It's a clear hot night, a three-quarter moon making the street lights insipid. There's more traffic than usual, the heat bringing out the party boys and drunkards.

On the corner of my street a hotted up four-wheel drive has hit the traffic light. The light pole is horizontal to the ground, the bull bar on the truck barely dented. The driver, checked shirt, shorts, thongs, is very impressed. He extols the virtues of his vehicle to a small crowd of interested onlookers. A police truck turns into the other end of the street, blue light turning slowly, as if it's too hot to really bother. It stops by the traffic light and a couple of uniforms get out.

My alley is deserted as I pull into it. In the garage one of the fluorescents needs a new tube. It flickers, distorting the shadows. There's a maroon sedan in the spot next to mine. A spot that's usually empty.

I fumble the keys at my door, dropping them. They scrape down the side of the jamb and tinkle gently on the carpet.

The second try is successful and I step into the flat. It feels odd, as if it's no longer mine and I'm just a visitor, a guest in someone else's life. He's sitting in the dark by the balcony, the curtain moving softly in the light breeze that blows in when the glass doors are open.

I push the door to behind me, leaving the lock on the snib. He doesn't speak until I snap the lights on.

"Took your time coming home, didn't you? Been out with the girlfriend, have you, Chief Inspector Stewart?"

"Hello, Mick. I wondered when you were going to turn up."

The anxiety and resentment that are his hallmarks in the office have left him here. Now he is confident and strong, clearly in control. This is a job he knows well. There's an automatic pistol with a long silencer on the barrel sitting in his lap. On the dining table sits a small black briefcase that isn't mine. I walk across to the table and put my briefcase next to his.

"What's in that, Mick? My bomb?"

"Yep. Made especially and all ready to go when I tell it to. There's not going to be very much left of you, ma'am."

I pull out a chair to sit down but he doesn't like that.

"Oh no you don't. You just stay standing until I tell you. Lift your shirt up."

I pull my shirt out of my pants and turn around slowly. Pulling my pants legs up I show him my ankles.

"No gun, Mick. You know I don't carry one."

"Just checking."

He stands up and comes across the room, the machine pistol in his left hand. I never realised he was left handed. He isn't, there's a knife in his right hand. He stands on the other side of the table and lifts the pistol, straight armed, until the barrel is right in front of my face.

"I've been waiting for this moment for a long time, bitch. A very long time and I intend to enjoy it."

"Did you make the bomb up yourself, Mick?"

"What? No. Ray gets them done by this bloke in forensic. Good eh. We blow you up and he comes in and studies his own bomb. The silly bugger has a gambling habit."

"Very clever. Can I get you a drink? I only have scotch, I'm not much of a drinker myself."

"Well, you wouldn't drink would you, control freak like you. Actually, I would like a scotch, Chief Inspector. Straight up."

I turn and walk into the kitchen. He follows, the gun up and close all the time. The liquor is in the cupboard over the stove. The glasses by the sink. He doesn't wait for a glass, just reaches across and takes the bottle, the knife back in his pocket. Then he pushes me back out to the living room, the gun jabbed against my ribs a couple of times to make me move faster. When I stop by the table, I turn my head just in time to see it coming. The scotch bottle catches me on the side of my temple.

When I fall, one of two ornate and heavy dining chairs catches me in the ribs. Rather tasteless antiques, like all the furnishings, they came with the flat. But Mick likes them. They have large arms and are heavy. Grabbing my collar he yanks me into the chair and snicks his handcuffs around my right wrist and the armrest. The scotch bottle sits on the table, the gun is still in his left hand.

Mick makes himself comfortable on the other side of the table. He sits in the chair that is twin to mine, puts the gun on the table out of my reach and in his, undoes the cap on the scotch and takes a drink. Blood is trickling down past my eye. Breathing is difficult, and there's fire in my ribs.

"So, what do you want to know, Jane? Ray said I could tell whatever you wanted to know. It's his gesture, his way of being generous."

Leaning back in the chair he spreads his arms, expansive, the man in command. I try to get on with it before the power goes to his head.

"Did Matthews have Mick Chambers killed?"

"What? No. Mick died skindiving. For real. He'd quit. He'd always wanted to live in the Solomons and when he had enough he got out. That's how Matthews got the system. Mick gave it to him. Still, Ray's built it up a lot since then. The real estate, that was all Ray's idea. Danelli was just a gopher back then. A small time dealer that Mick had been using to flog his stuff. Faggots are a good market."

"Did Matthews know Danelli and Sean Porter were going to do Ryan?"

"No. Boy, was he pissed off when he found out. Sean was always a greedy little shit. Matthews should have put him away years ago but he kept Danelli happy. Where is he anyway? Matthews is convinced you've got him tucked away somewhere but I can't see it myself. Why would you take him and leave Danelli? Nah, I think the little scroat has buggered off somewhere. Probably found a better fuck."

He takes a swig from the scotch, tipping the bottle back, his adam's apple working as he swallows

"Why did Danelli owe Matthews money?"

"Nosy cunt. Recording all this are you? Not that it matters. Nothing's going to be left of this place and there are no arselicking goody twoshoes here to save you."

"Why did Danelli owe Matthews money?"

"What makes you so sure he did, Miss Hotshot Detective?

"Because they went to Ryan Porter looking for money. Something must have gone wrong. The system must have been running for years. Why did they need money now?"

"Yeah, well. Danelli lost a deal. He said the drop was short when he went to pick it up in that stupid boat of his but Ray reckons he sold it on. Some stuff the same quality turned up with another dealer a couple of weeks later. So Ray told him to get the cash for it or he'd have Sean knocked. Boy, did he panic."

He takes another swig. More than a couple of sentences and he gets thirsty.

"How does Matthews get the stuff into the country?"

"Boats mostly. Freighters drop it over the side when they come down the coast. He's got some mules too, I think, who come in through the airports. His daughter recruits them from uni. It's a real family business. And he's not going to lose it just because of some greedy kid and a smart cunt. They never should have let cunts like you in the force. There's always going to be dealers and dope. Better that it's us than some nasty little Lebbo bastard. As least we keep the business under control."

My back aches and the cuffs are cutting my wrist. I want to urinate. I shift in the chair. The gun comes up off the table, he rises out of his chair and whips the barrel across the right side of my face. My chair rocks back against the wall but doesn't fall. There is blood in my mouth. He laughs, sits back and looks around the room. I never thought he could move so fast.

"You've got shit taste in furnishings. Surprising really. I would have thought someone like you, always so well dressed and neat, would have a better place. Never can tell, can you. Eva wanted this job. She's heard me bitch about you for the last eighteen months and finally wanted to meet you. But, nope. This one I wanted."

"Who's Eva?"

"My wife. Real smart. Goes to uni with Christine, Ray's girl."

"She did Danelli."

"How did you know that?"

He gets out of the chair and leans over me, across the table, shoulders hunched, face bellicose with the alcohol. The level in the bottle has dropped considerably.

"How did you fucking know that, bitch?"

He grabs my hair and pulls me up into his face. I can smell the scotch and the garlic he had for dinner.

"You fucking tell me how you know that, you fucking cunt, or I'll fucking cut you."

I'm pulled out of the chair, its weight cutting off the circulation in my right wrist, dragging at my shoulder. My vision blurs and my face throbs. My head is ringing like an empty drum. The edge of the table catches my ribs. He has the knife again. In his right hand. Out of the corner of my right eye I can see blood and skin on the sight at the end of the gun barrel where it sits next to the bottle.

A giant moth has come in through the balcony door. It throws itself against the light. Violent shadows box across the room. Coburn's face flickers in and out of darkness. He has the knife on my cheek under my left eye.

"I've cut women before, you know. You might be going to die, cunt, but you're going to hurt like hell before you get there. I took a woman's nipples off once. Talk about a scream. Of course, I fucked her first."

His eyes are pale blue and inches from mine. The whites are bloodshot and muddy. His face is hazy at the corners as if I am looking through a vaselined lens. A pulse beats beneath the florid skin of his cheek. But he's not quite ready yet. He shoves me back again. This time I help the chair and it falls completely. I'm under the table lying on my right arm. I can see his feet moving back and there it is, just where Fargo left it. I reach up and rip my revolver out of the tape holding it under the table. But I'm not much of a shot with my right hand let alone my left.

I hit him in the thigh and he falls on his buttocks, right hand gripping his leg. Blood is spouting from under his fingers, very fast and very red. The table obscures his shoulders and head but I can see the pistol coming down in his left hand. It swings towards me. I fire again and miss. The third shot catches him in the chest and knocks him back, flat onto the floor.

When Fargo bursts through the door Coburn and I are lying under the table like a pair of drunks. Except that he's dead as well.

Fargo takes a while, far too long, to find the keys to Coburn's cuffs. When I finally get to go to the bathroom my ribs are so sore I can hardly do a thing. There's another gun in here, inside the dryer. Fargo collects it when I've finished, along with the one under the pillow and the one in the freezer.

I wash down a couple of Panadene Forte with some of the scotch. It makes me gag which doesn't help my ribs either. Fargo lights a rollie.

"Jesus, boss, you sure like to do things the easy way."

Then he calls Cameron and tells her to come up. She looks troubled when she sees my face but doesn't mention it. She just says that the tape worked and we got Coburn telling his story. Fargo and I get up to leave.

"Give us time to get there, Alice, then call the local uniforms and the bomb squad. For all we know Matthews has got someone who reports any local activity. Give us about forty minutes. If any of the neighbours have called about the gunshots just stall as long as you can. "

She looks at me.

"Are you sure you're alright to go? You look a bit of a mess."

"I'm fine."

By the time we get going the four-wheel drive has gone and now there is just the bent traffic light left to tell its story. The sky is orange with street light.

In the rear view mirror my face is swelling, my cut cheek turning blue. I wipe off as much of the blood as I can while Fargo drives. The streets are empty and hot. We could be driving through a forsaken city, an urban *Marie Celeste*. A couple of miles from Matthews' house we pull into a twenty-four hour gas station. Fargo talks to the occupants of a battered blue van waiting, lonely, on the apron and when we leave, they swing in behind us.

On Matthews' street the houses are all dark, still asleep and quiet. As I get out of the car in front of the discreetly careful house my ribs catch and for a moment I can't breathe. Fargo sees it and starts to say something but thinks better of it.

We wait while the personnel from the van deploy around the house, "Police" gleaming whitely on their backs in the early light. There is no sound, no radios squawk, no voices call. The silence is almost solid, palpable. I walk up the front path, Fargo behind me.

I know as soon as I knock on the door. There is a particular feel to the front door of an empty house. It takes Special Weapons a while to get it open and in the end, they have to use an oxy torch. It looks like an ordinary door but then it looks like an ordinary house. Fargo is impatient with the door and looks for a window. They are all barred and the back door appears to be as solid as the front one.

Inside everything is carefully discreet. The furniture is good quality, nothing flashy, nothing overt. Solid, suburban. There is a small office off the main bedroom. The computer has been smashed and there isn't a single scrap of paper. Dust marks the rosewood shelves where documents have been removed. The retreat was orderly. Wardrobes are closed and drawers shut. They've left a lot of household stuff.

The neighbours, sleepy and irritated, never heard anything, didn't know they were going, what a shock.

I'm very tired.

I write a report, a full one, telling as much of the story as I can bear to. I send it to the Area Commander with copies to the State Commander and the Commissioner. There will be an inquiry. I get a message that the Commissioner wants to see me but I don't go.

I have the strangest sensation that I am going deaf. At work I see people speaking to me, see their mouths moving but I hardly hear a thing. Staff troop through my office, make their reports, assess their cases and I don't have the least idea what they are telling me. A miasma of fatigue and depression hangs around me, a noxious fog of despair and self-contempt.

I get a visit from IAD. They're still chasing the allegation that I'm having an affair with Valentine. I tell them the truth. They begin to be aggressive but Fargo and Cameron come into my office like a pair of body guards and they desist, threatening departmental charges before they leave.

Coburn's body lies at the morgue in Glebe. No one claims it. It seems Eva went with the Matthews family.

I wait until after Sam's funeral to resign. He is given full honours and I want to salute him.

Valentine

Three magpies scratch behind me as I hoe. They step carefully across the uneven dirt, beaks pushing clods aside. Dignified and busy. The magpie is an industrious bird, diligent and concentrated, always pottering about amongst the vegies. This morning I can see no other fauna. There is fog. Unusual for this time of year. A white blanket, damp and dense. The river is solid in its silence. Even if there are boats out there the wet air absorbs the engine sounds. I can't even see my house from down here.

I like the fog, it is safe and sheltering. I can work here in this moist cocoon and wound myself thinking about the girl I've lost. She rides like an ache just below my breastbone, a hard lump of loneliness.

My lovely dogs are pushing around in the bush. I can't see them but I can hear the undergrowth being snapped and pushed aside. Whoever started the myth that animals are quiet in the bush didn't know what they were talking about. They crash and bash about like demented bulldozers. The only time they're silent is when they're asleep.

The basil is beginning to flower. Pesto time. I can sell it to the weekenders for $5 a jar. They love it. The fog has left tiny droplets shimmering on the bright green leaves. I won't pick them today. The thought of gathering the leaves and chopping the garlic is more than I can bear.

The magpies have turned their attention to the curry plants. They are poking around in the stems. Their action releases a hot perfume into the air at odds with the morning dampness.

A dog barks and then they all run off through the fog. I should make the pesto today, I'm just being a lazy bitch. If I don't make it today then it will be next week before I get to it and by then the basil will have flowered and the stems and leaves will be that much coarser. Work, you stupid cow, instead of moping about the place like some kind of morose adolescent.

I will find my sanity again. In the earth, the animals and the yeast. Where it has always been. I will study the open skies.

Stewart

I drive north, the few possessions I can be bothered with jumbled on the back seat of the car. There is a four-lane bridge where the road crosses the river. Just before it is the turnoff. The car seems to swing on to the road between the river and the railway line all by itself. There's a for sale sign on the Masterson house.

I park beside the marina and walk out on the dock. A small ferry comes into the wharf and a gaggle of schoolchildren disembark. Noisy and self-absorbed, they clatter along the pontoons then disappear down the road towards the railway station. Three men in flapping check shirts and thongs are loading cartons of beer and fishing rods into a hire boat.

Cameron's little boat bobs in a new berth waiting for its new owner. The river whispers around me like my own indecision. It's early on a Tuesday morning. She'll be making her deliveries.

For eighteen years I have been a police officer and nothing else. And now it's gone, lost with Coburn's blood on the rented carpet of my rented flat. Gone with Matthews and his corruption. Gone in the bomb that killed Sam and Danelli. Gone with IAD and their allegations of misconduct. Gone in my own misjudgments and errors. Eighteen years that trail, empty and exhausted, behind me.

My ribs are bruised and sore, aching with every step. Lassitude has melted my bones. Telling myself I'm just depressed and it will all pass does little to help. Every thought, every movement seems to require twice as much effort as it should.

The richness, the complexities and the joy I have so recently found came with my wild river girl. And who's to say whose morals are preferable — hers in their practical simplicity or mine, enmeshed in a corrupt system, inept and unresolved?

I can see her island, blue in the morning light. The river, muddy and brown, stretches out from here to there. Sometimes it all seems so simple but underneath that brown surface are so many currents, so many dangers.

I only have to wait about half an hour before the tinnie appears around the point going faster than it should. The boat roars down the channel despite the no wash zone and swings into the wharf. She slips the ropes onto the bollards, economy and grace.

For a brief moment, when she first sees me, hope flares up in her face, then just as quickly fades. All the defences are up.

"Jane. Hi."

Her singlet has rucked up over the sheath knife she always wears on her hip. I wonder if forensic would ever have found Masterson's blood on it. For a moment I can't say anything. She looks so strong and sure, free of the virus of self-doubt and contempt.

"I'm ah … I'm going away for a while. I've resigned. I'm just … I need some time. To consider things."

"Are you coming back?"

In that simple question, which she asks with such clear hope, I find my own answer. And with it the first stirring, a subtle shift in the load I have forced myself to carry. Is it courage or simply inevitability? I have so much joy and so much pain wrapped up in her.

"Perhaps. Maybe. Probably."

She rubs her bare foot on the rough planking. Then reaches out with her hand and very gently traces the stitches in my cheek. She smiles, sweet and a little sad.

"I'm not going anywhere if you want to find me. Keep up the swimming."

I turn away and walk back to the car.

The *Annie Marie* is tied to my wharf. She is a splendid boat. A bold and handsome craft. All brass and twinkles in the late afternoon sun. For Ryan and Ted this boat was everything. It kept the world at bay. While there was an *Annie Marie* there was always escape. A safety hatch to a better place.

Ted is trying to get rid of Rosie but she won't go. She has sat, impassive and stubborn on the rear deck. He is trying to push her off but she has her front feet firmly against the scuppers. It's an unequal battle. She weighs more than he does.

He turns to me, helpless, frustration and despair racing wet down his cheeks. It has never healed, the hole that Ryan left. A great, gaping pain is all that Ted can feel. His soul is an empty beach under an icy wind. My old friend is going to end it. He is going to take his beautiful boat out to sea, open her stopcocks and wait for Ryan to join him. He is going to meet his love.

I free the line from the for'ard bollard and walk back to Rosie. I reach up and put my arm around her middle. As I lift her off I push the heavy boat out with my foot. It slowly slides away from the wharf. Rosie struggles and I drop her. For a moment I think she is going to jump back but the launch has moved too far.

Ted spins the wheel and eases the throttles up. I slip down into my kayak and paddle out behind him. Rosie jumps in the water, swimming after us. I have to hit her on the nose with my paddle to make her turn around.

She struggles back onto the pontoon and sits down. Lifting her nose to the sky she begins to howl. The others join in.

As Ted takes his boat down to the ocean, I paddle behind him. He was a friend. He deserves a farewell. The dogs' chorus echoes through the red cliffs until we have gone too far to hear it.

The swell grows as we leave the river. And there before us, around the point, is the rolling sea. A few late fishing boats straggle back towards the sunset. I keep pace with him for another kilometre but then he opens her up and she is too fast for me. I wave but he doesn't look back.

BlackWattle Press Books

KIRSTY MACHON

Immortality

ISBN 1 875243 22 4 - 128 pages - Aust RRP $14.95

delicious, dangerous ... and deadly — *I lay masturbating on the couch, dreaming of the statue of liberty. Just because I don't have a body doesn't mean I can't enjoy pleasure. It's the liberation from the finality of orgasm that makes my existence a hundred times more pleasurable…* A young boy falls in love with his golden haired brother. A jilted ghost with gallows humour plots the ultimate revenge from beyond the grave. Jackie Traval finds the body of a murdered weather girl, and for the first time is in love. And an ex–rentboy contemplates (im)mortality high above the seductive sea. In these twelve stories about death, Kirsty Machon writes of the darkness and sunlight, of gender and the flesh. The resonances of earthly and deathly desire are explored through the eyes of the victims, of those left behind ... and a phantom victor from the other side.

Reviews -'It's hot. It's steamy. It's black. It's witty. It's got balls. It's got cunt. It's got what it takes. It's queer Sydney. Buy it!' -Michael Chapman, Sydney Star Observer. 'There is nothing ordinary about Immortality.*' -Campaign*

PHILLIP SCOTT

One Dead Diva

ISBN 1 875243 21 6 - 230 pages - Aust RRP $16.95

Jennifer Burke was a rising star in the Sydney City Opera until she fell off a cliff ... or was she pushed? Marc, an accident-prone opera queen, and his friend Paul, a chorus boy addicted to dance parties, decide to investigate. Being very amateur detectives, they incompetently lose the evidence and accuse all the wrong people in their quest to solve the puzzle. Part murder mystery, part farce, part contemporary satire, and even part romance, *One Dead Diva* is one lively read.

Reviews - 'beautifully executed comic set-pieces a genuinely funny book' - Sydney Star Observer. 'twists through farce, flirts with romance, dallies with death, it's good writing and very entertaining.' -Michael Hurley, Campaign.

BlackWattle Press Books

GINA SCHIEN

Timing the Heart

ISBN 1 875243 20 8 - 160 pages - Aust RRP $14.95

Bonnie loves drums, music and women. She believes that one day she'll play in the perfect band and have the ideal girlfriend. For a while it seems possible, but in the early '80s, the music industry didn't much like dykes with short hair. Bonnie has to negotiate half-open closets, prying gossip writers, and a broken heart before she can learn the real art of playing. Timing the Heart is a story about lesbian sex, growing up, living with your girlfriend's children, and finding a sound engineer with principles.

Reviews - 'an unpretentious and satisfying novel from one of Australia's most gifted lesbian writers,' -Julia Hancock, Lesbians on the Loose. 'enjoyable and thought-provoking,' -Jan Percival, Bliss. 'engaging warmth and irony,' -Robert Johnston, Campaign.

JOHN LONIE

Acts of Love

ISBN 1 875243 23 2 - 224 pages - Aust RRP $16.95

Three acts of love – In *Friend of Dorothy,* a boy leaves home. It's southern Queensland in the early 70s and Adrian lives in a paradise of rainforests and empty beaches; he's young and alive with a raw instinct for sex but not for who he really is. – Leo Day, TV star, finally meets Mr Right while on holidays in Los Angeles, fulfilling his Aunt Effie's prophesy, 'You will meet a man, and he will change your life.' *Que Sera Sera* is a story of the path from lust to true love. – In *The Story of Harold Friday,* 'Lucky' Friday was the youngest in the platoon at war on Bougainville in 1945 and was overwhelmed and taken, not by a bullet, but by love. Now, on Anzac Day 50 years later, Harold is set to confront the consequences of that love.

Reviews - 'immensely readble, cleverly crafted and emotionally frank. Unreservedly recommended.' -Graeme Aitken, OutRage. 'a fabulous read: funny sweet, poignant and sad in just the right combination.' -Zoë Velonis, Brother Sister.

BlackWattle Press Books

GARY DUNNE

Shadows On The Dance Floor

ISBN 1 875243 11 9 - 96 pages Aust RRP $13.95

"Where there's hair, there's hope," states Mr Pointy Head, inner-city survivor, shoplifter and owner of three milk crates of second hand mens' underpants. Back in 1985 he and his ex-boyfriend Grace went for HIV blood tests together. It's now 1991 and, for the first time their different results really begin to matter. Nothing that Gary Dunne has previously written will prepare you for the hilarious yet poignant intensity of *Shadows On The Dance Floor*. It's an insider's story of a community where illness and death are common aspects of day to day living. With its dry wit and humour this novel powerfully captures an Australian response to AIDS.

Reviews - 'Regrettably familiar territory with sincerity, simplicity and devilish lashings of humour' -Robert Johnston, Campaign. 'Brittle and extremely camp, a tough comic novel' -Australian Book Review.

BlackWattle Books are available at bookshops everywhere, please ask.

or write to **BlackWattle Press Pty Ltd**
PO Box 142, Broadway NSW Australia 2007
Phone & fax - Sydney 02 **9212 3047**
Australia +612 9212 3047

For the latest information on our products visit our web site at:
http://www.pinkboard.net.au/~blackwattle

or E-mail us at: **blackwattle@geko.com.au**

If you're ordering from us directly, we accept Visa/Master/Bankcard, please include $2 per book pp (Australia/NZ) and $4 per book pp (elsewhere)

Distributed in Australia, and New Zealand by -
Australian Book Group, Phone 056 25 4290 or Fax 056 25 4272
Sales representitives in all states.
Distributed in the United States of America, and Canada by -
InBook, part of the LPC Group, Chicago, IL
Phone 1 800 243 0138 or fax 1 800 334 3892
Distributed in the United Kingdom, and Europe by -
Turnaround Publisher Services, London N22
Phone 0181 829 3000 or fax 0181 88 150 88

RRP - Australian prices listed are Recommended Retail Prices only
BlackWattle Press Pty Ltd ACN 061 418 433